I0724080

catgirl doctor

Volume 3

By Brandon Varnell
Art by Liremi

Catgirl Doctor, Vol. 3

If you'd like to know when I'm releasing a new book, you can sign up for my mailing list at https://www.varnell-brandon.com/mailing-list.

ISBN: 978-1-951904-89-0 (Paperback)
978-1-951904-88-3 (eBook)

dedication

This page is made in dedication to my amazing patrons. Without them, my characters would never get lewded by so many wonderful artists:

Aaron Harris; Abraham Madsen; Adam; Alarinnise; Alex Burt; Arnando Pastrana; Arron Cortrighr; Austin; Brendan Smiley; Brennan; Bruce Johnson; Bryce McClay; ByzFan; Casey G. May; Catcrazy9; Chace Corso; Charles Dorfeuille; Chett Nialo; Christopher Gross; Cody Woodard; CosmicOrange; Daniel Glasson; David Bell; Edward Grindle; Edward Lamar Stephenson; Edward P Warmouth; ElJako98; Emery Moore; Erik Bailey; Feitochan; Forrest Hansen; Forest Hansen; IronKing; Jacob Flores; Jason Wilcox; Jeremy Schultz; Jessy Torres; Jesus De Guzman; John Patton; Jordan McDonald; Joseph Snyder; Josh Bunton; Joshua Kern; Lucid Fayt; Mark Frabotta; Mason; Matthew Wallace; Max A Kramer; Michael Erwin; Michael Moneymaker; Mike Dennehy; MrRedSkill; Nathan S; Norodim; Nyxtarrynne; Phoenixblue; Philip Hedgepeth; Rafael; Randgofire23; Raymond T; Red Phoenix; Reent Dopychai; Repooc llahsram; Richard Garret; Rob Hammel; Robert Shofner; Rooser45; Roy Cales; Samuel Donaldson; Sean Gray; Seismic Wolf; Smudi Corp; Synn Shadow; Tanner Lovelace; Thomas Jackson; Thomas Lindsay; Thomas Oconnell; Tora Linkley; Travis Cox; Vincent Frosceno; William Crew; Wizard4Hire; Xpectation; xy172; Zach Miller; Zach Strickland; Zak Whiteaker; Zenn Barger

table of contents

Chapter 1

CHRIS'S AWAKENING WAS a slow process, his mind coming to after being lost within a fuzzy haze. He opened his eyes to find a ceiling above him, covered by strands of black and silver streamers… or so he thought at first. It wasn't until he felt the warmth of two bodies, one large and one petite, on his left and right sides, that he realized he was seeing hair.

He turned his head to the left. The long silver hair and pale skin of Silva met his vision. Her eyes were closed, pink lips gently parted as a soft whistling sound escaped from her mouth. She was snuggling her petite body against his side, her small breasts rubbing his skin, nipples erect as if from the cold. As he watched her, Silva shifted, raising her leg, which brushed against his fully erect cock.

"Hnn…"

A soft hiss escaped his lips as electricity raced through his nerves, but he tried to push his arousal back.

His dick felt like it had been rubbed raw. Last night, he, Kuro, and Silva had a threesome, and it had been the most epic experience of his life, but it had also left him more than a little exhausted and… worn, he guessed would be a good word for it. He didn't think he wanted to have sex right now.

Once he had confirmed that Silva was on his left, he looked toward his right, where Kuro was snuggling with him. She was much taller than he was, so she wasn't using his head as a pillow like Silva. Her head was above him, nose buried in his hair, tits pressed against his head. From his position, Chris felt the woman's hard muscles rubbing his arm. It was an interesting experience. He'd never slept with a woman who was more muscular than him before.

With both of them clinging to him, Chris realized he probably wasn't going to be able to get out of their embrace any time soon. He was just about to let himself fall back asleep. However, before he shut his eyes, a vivid blue color made him look toward the head of the bed, where he found a blonde-haired, blue-eyed beauty with cat ears glaring at him.

"Elsa…"

"You look pretty cozy," Elsa muttered bitterly. "It

sounded like you three had a great time last night without me."

Chris felt his heart quiver at the hurt in her voice. He recalled Elsa's confession several days ago when they were working on creating the GoFundMe page for Sister Ann, her admittance that she had always seen him as potential mate material and not an older brother like he'd assumed. Back then, he had asked her to give him time.

He wondered if his time had now run out.

"I'm sorry," Chris muttered.

"You shouldn't… apologize if you're not going to do anything to make things right," Elsa muttered. "I… you know how I feel about you, and yet, not only are you sleeping with Silva, but you're sleeping with Kuro now too? How am I supposed to feel about this? Am I not good enough?"

"That isn't it," Chris said as he tried to get out of Kuro's hold, but he found such a task impossible. She seemed to sense him trying to leave and curled her body around his. Her legs entwined through his, locking them in place, and her arms pulled his head closer to her, keeping him pinned.

Kuro was ridiculously strong. He didn't know how

this woman became so damn powerful, but her physical strength easily exceeded his. There was no way he could escape her grip unless she let him.

Elsa's glare hardened. "The hell it isn't. What am I supposed to think when you add another catgirl to your harem before me?"

Chris winced, but Elsa quickly spun around and ran out of the room, leaving him with the two sleeping catgirls. But unlike when he woke up, Chris couldn't find comfort in their embrace, his mind replaying the scene just now over and over.

"Maybe… it wasn't a good idea to sleep with Kuro right now," a voice said in his left ear. It was Silva, eyes open a crack as she stared at him. Her blue and golden heterochromatic eyes gazed into his with an apologetic expression. "I'm sorry. I think I should have been less accepting of this and asked Kuro to wait for you to fix things with Elsa."

He thought about that for a moment, then slowly shook his head. "No… had nothing like this happened, I probably would have dragged out this issue with Elsa for much longer. With this, I now have to do something, or else she'll stay mad and hurt."

Silva nodded as if she understood my line of

thinking. "In that case, let me switch places with you. You go and talk to Elsa."

"Thank you," Chris murmured, staring into Silva's eyes before he placed a hand under her chin and tilted her head up. He kissed her on the lips, letting his mouth linger over hers, enjoying her subtle taste.

He pulled back and maneuvered himself around Silva, who seamlessly inserted herself between him and Kuro. The larger catgirl shifted as if she could sense their movement. However, seconds later, she wound her dark arms around the much smaller Silva and was cuddling with the tiny catgirl instead of him.

After Chris climbed out of the bed, he turned around and gazed at the two. They were naked as the day they were born, their limbs entwined together, Silva's head resting on Kuro's massive breasts. The black and white combination of their skin created a striking contrast. Their beauty was so different from each other. Silva was an innocent-looking beauty who seemed very pure, like unblemished snow, while Kuro had the beauty of an Amazonian queen with the strength to match. Both were gorgeous in different ways, and it was that dichotomy that made this sight so arousing. Truth be told, Chris could have stayed there for hours and just admired them.

He sighed and wandered over to his drawer, taking out a pair of boxers that he put on, then, after a moment's thought, a pair of sweatpants. Chris didn't know if it would be appropriate to wander around in front of Elsa in his boxers. He used to do it all the time back when they were younger. She'd just been another member of the family, but now…

He shook his head.

Elsa was exactly where he figured she would be, sitting on the couch with her knees drawn up to her chest. She was wearing simple yellow pajamas. The long sleeves of her shirt had cute frills along the cuffs. She was wearing shorts instead of pants. As his gaze traveled along the expanse of her milky legs, Chris wondered if maybe it was her confession that caused him to realize how gorgeous she was… but no. He had always known she was pretty and merely refused to acknowledge it back then.

One of the more interesting features of Elsa as she sat in this position was definitely her chest. Because her boobs were so large, as she sat there, hugging her knees, they spilled out of the sides, straining against the shirt. He wouldn't be surprised if some of her buttons started popping off if she kept this position. It looked like her breasts were causing the seams to strain.

He wandered over to her and sat down. They didn't speak for a while, but that was because Chris couldn't figure out what he should say. What did someone say in a situation like this? Well, if he was a harem protagonist from one of those anime he watched, he'd act like an oblivious idiot who didn't know when a woman was in love with him, but he was sure even someone as dumb as Ichika Orimura would be unable to keep acting oblivious in this instance.

"I'm sorry," he apologized. "I know this is hard. I know I'm hurting you. I… if I was a better person, or maybe if I was more capable, I would be able to say or do something that would make this all better… but I'm not. I don't know what I'm supposed to do in this situation."

Elsa didn't say anything for a moment, then sighed. "You always were the type to apologize first. I don't want your apology. All I want is for you to love me… like you love those two. Is that too much to ask?"

What an incredibly hard-to-answer question.

Chris placed his hands on either side of him, fingers grasping the soft fabric of his couch as he leaned back and looked at the ceiling. His mind raced. How should he answer this?

"It's not… too much to ask, but you know it's also gonna take time." He paused and tried to sort his thoughts. "Silva and Kuro have only recently come into my life. We had no relationship prior to the one we have now. But you're different. You were raised alongside me as a member of my family, and I've thought of you as a sister for so long now that changing my way of thinking is going to take a long time."

"How long will it take?" asked Elsa. Chris made the mistake of glancing at her face. Her eyes were slightly red, which made his stomach clench. He looked away again.

"I don't know." Chris shrugged. "But you have to understand, I do love you. I really, really love you. I love you so much that I'm going to do my best to accept you as a catpanion and not the sister I've been seeing you as for the past twelve years."

"I know all that, but I just… I hate not being a part of that." Elsa raised a hand and gestured toward the wall behind them. The bedroom was on the other side of that wall. "I want to share kisses with you, to sleep with you, to be with you. I want to have what they have right now.

I've waited for years for you to notice me. It really sucks that even after all this time, you still haven't done so. Worse still, two catgirls have beaten me to the punch."

Chris had known ever since her confession that he had been hurting her with his ignorance, that he'd been causing her pain. That knowledge caused his heart to throb painfully in his chest. It felt like cracks were appearing in his heart. Even so, he would never let his pain show, because he knew that what he felt now didn't compare to what Elsa had been feeling this whole time.

Chris made a decision. Screw taking his time, screw waffling in indecision. He was fixing this now. He wasn't going to let someone so precious to him suffer like this. Not anymore.

Scooting closer, Chris reached out and pulled Elsa to him. She squeaked and unwrapped her arms from around her legs. Her feet would have fallen to the floor, but he hooked his arms underneath her knees and shifted them so she was sitting lengthwise across his lap. Then he wrapped his arms around her waist and pulled her close.

Elsa was so shocked she could do nothing but rest her head on his shoulder.

They remained like that for some time, silence

elapsing between them. It was broken by Elsa.

"Chris?"

Her words caused him to look down, into Elsa's beautiful blue eyes, which were always open and honest, showing exactly what she was feeling at any given moment. He reached out with a tentative hand and stroked her cheek. Elsa was startled, but before she could fully comprehend what was happening, he began stroking the spot just underneath her chin.

A soft purr emitted from the back of Elsa's throat as she tilted her head to grant him better access. She closed her eyes, ears twitching, tail curling. Even her toes were clenching and unclenching from the pleasure coursing through her body.

"This isn't fair," she muttered softly. "Using my weakness against me... nya..."

"Elsa, I promise that I am going to do right by you, which is why... I'm going to register you as my catpanion later today," Chris said.

"R-really?" Elsa looked up, startled.

"Really." Chris nodded.

Tears emerged from Elsa's eyes as she buried her face into his neck. He could feel the wetness flowing down his skin, but that only caused him to hold her more tightly.

"I'm so happy," Elsa muttered. "I… I'm…"

She trailed off. Chris wondered why for a moment, but then she began sniffing him. After a moment, she pulled back and stared at his face, her nose wrinkling.

"You smell," she declared.

Chris snorted with laughter. "I'll go take a shower then."

"That's a good idea."

Elsa climbed off his lap, allowing Chris to get back on his feet and make his way to the bathroom. He closed the door behind him, though he didn't lock it, and stripped off his sweats and boxers before turning on the water. He relieved himself while the shower was heating up. As he flushed the toilet, he reached a hand into the shower and waited for the water to heat up, then stepped in.

The hot spray was nice. It caused his aching body and sore muscles to relax. He really was sore.

Last night was the first time Chris had ever had a threesome. He now realized how difficult it was to keep up with two catgirls. Chris had pushed himself last night to please Silva and Kuro, but perhaps he had gone a little overboard.

As these thoughts filled his mind, the door opened and Silva walked in. She was still completely naked. Chris sucked in a deep breath as he stared at her small breasts and bare pussy, then at her perfectly round ass as she turned around and closed the door. Unlike him, she actually locked the door before moving over to the shower.

"Can I join you?" she asked.

He shrugged. "Would you leave if I said no?"

"Yes… but I really don't want to leave."

"Then I guess it's a good thing I don't want you to either." He smiled. "Come on in."

Silva pulled back the clear curtains and stepped into the shower behind him. She didn't say anything as she grabbed a bottle of soap, squirted some onto her hands, and began washing his back. Her soft hands were like heaven. She not only washed his back, but she kneaded the muscles as if working out the knots. It felt so good that his legs almost turned to jelly.

"Is everything okay with Elsa?" asked Silva as she knelt behind him and began washing his legs too.

"I think so," Chris said, then paused. "I'm going to register her and Kuro as my catpanions today."

"I think that's a good idea," Silva admitted. "I

know Kuro will be happy, even if she doesn't admit it out loud."

Chris nodded as Silva stood back up, pressed her small chest against his back, and reached around him to begin washing his front. The way her nipples rubbed him made Chris wish he could get his dick up. However, it was still feeling the effects of the previous night.

When Silva finished washing him, it was his turn. He used the shampoo and bathing cap to wash her hair and ears, gently massaging her scalp in ways that made Silva purr with pleasure. After her hair was clean, he used a floral-scented soap to clean her body, working his hands over her breasts, watching as Silva closed her eyes and released more pleased purrs.

He focused on her breasts for a moment, watching as her small nipples became puffy and stiff. The water dripping down her body caused her pure white skin to glisten. Part of him wished he was those water droplets. He was tempted to lean down and suck one of those nipples into his mouth.

As he was kneeling in front of her to clean her legs, Chris found himself staring at her pussy. Water was dripping from it and down her thighs. He wanted so badly to pressed his lips to her pussy, push his tongue into her folds, and explore her depths, but he held himself back. Now was not that time. He leaned forward and kissed only her stomach before he finished cleaning her off.

Silva smiled as if she understood what he really wanted to do.

Once they were clean, Chris did what he always did, helping her dry off, then drying and combing her hair with a blow dryer and a comb specifically made for catgirls.

They eventually emerged from the shower and walked into the living room. Kuro was awake, as he suspected since Silva was awake, though she still looked tired as she sat at the table with half-lidded eyes. She looked up when they walked in and smiled.

"That was an awfully long time in the shower," she commented.

Chris shrugged. "We like to be thorough."

She snorted. "I bet." Standing up, Kuro made her way toward the shower. "I should take a shower too. I'll be out in a bit."

"Breakfast should be ready by the time you're done," Chris said.

Kuro waved her hand as she walked past them,

entered the bathroom, and closed the door behind her.

Chris decided to make some breakfast for everyone. While Silva went over to sit on the couch beside Elsa, he went into the kitchen and checked the fridge. After confirming the ingredients they had on hand, he decided on what he was going to make.

A frittata.

He was cooking for four people, and one of them was a big catgirl with a lot of muscles, so he needed to use more ingredients than usual to make it. He used all twelve of his remaining eggs, half a cup of heavy cream, and two cups of cheddar cheese.

Taking his nonstick skillet, he placed it on the stove before turning on the oven and heating it to 400 degrees. He whisked the eggs and cream together in a large bowl, added salt to taste, and set it aside. Chris cooked the bacon in his pan after. A loud sizzling sound soon emitted from the pan as the scents of bacon grease and fat filled the air. It took about eight minutes for the bacon to become crispy, then he set it aside on a plate lined with paper towels.

The next step was sauteing the potatoes in the bacon fat, which he did while seasoning it with a sprinkling of pepper and more salt, then piled spinach into the pan alongside garlic and thyme. He stirred until the spinach wilted before adding the cheese, and then finally, poured the egg mixture into the skillet and baked the whole concoction into the oven.

As he finished that last step, he looked into the living room and saw Silva and Elsa chatting about something. He didn't know what they were talking about, but his heart eased when he saw the smiles they were both wearing. It was good to see them getting along, and it was even better to see Elsa no longer looking sad. He didn't ever want to see that look on her face again.

Kuro arrived in the living room, dressed in her normal carpenter pants and sleeveless muscle shirt. She joined Silva and Elsa, though all of them soon stopped talking as Chris removed the frittata from the oven. They sniffed the air as the scent of his cooking washed over them.

Silva was the first to react. She stood up, walked over to him, and began helping Chris set the table. She got out hot pads and placed them on the table so he could set the frittata down, then added placemats, plates, napkins, and forks and knives on the table for everyone.

"Thanks," Chris said.

Silva smiled at him.

During breakfast, Chris explained his plans for them, how he was going to register Kuro and Elsa as his catpanions. While Elsa was beaming at the idea, Kuro was looking pensive. He didn't expect that and asked if something was wrong.

"There's nothing wrong." She shook her head. "I guess the idea of becoming a registered catpanion just… isn't something I'm used to. Honestly, the idea that we would make this official never even occurred to me."

"Are you against it?" asked Chris.

Kuro needed a moment before answering him. "No… I'm not against it. I actually appreciate that you want me to register as your catpanion. It's just going to take some getting used to. Also," she smirked at him as she added, "I don't want you to think I'm going to move in with you just because I'm your catpanion."

"Do you still intend to live at Sister Ann's orphanage?" asked Silva with a curious tilt of her head.

"I do." Kuro nodded. "Someone has to look after Lin, Lacy, Elizabeth, Catherine, and Maddison."

None of them could disagree with her words. They all knew that Kuro was kind of like the mother figure among the catgirls who'd been abused by Markus, and she wouldn't feel right abandoning them to come live with Chris, Silva, and Elsa. If nothing else, she wanted to help them out until they could choose what they wanted to do with their lives. She told them as much, and they accepted it.

Breakfast was soon finished, the table was cleared, and the dishes were cleaned. Chris was told to sit back by all three catgirls. Meanwhile, Kuro cleared the table while Silva washed the dishes and Elsa dried them. Once they were done, the four of them left the apartment and hopped onto a bus.

Their destination was the Catgirl Protection Bureau Office of Catpanion and Child Registration.

Chris and Silva had already been there recently, but Kuro and Elsa had not, and they looked around as they entered the front lobby.

The last time he and Silva were there, a young couple with four children had been present. No one else was inside this time. Well, no one except for the receptionist sitting behind the desk. It was the same blonde catgirl from before. As they entered, the catgirl looked up from her desk, smiled, and then her eyes widened when she recognized him and Silva.

"You two are back," she exclaimed, then looked at

Kuro and Elsa. Her smile went from professional to catlike and sly. "I see you have two more catgirls with you. Does this mean you're here to register them both as your catpanions?"

"It does," Chris said.

"Very well." The catgirl typed away at her computer, then looked at Elsa and Kuro. "I'll need your names please."

"Elsa Redford."

"Kuro Sterkrou."

The catgirl typed the names in, then nodded. "I have both of your names on file here. There are no problems with Ms. Redford's files, but..." Kuro stiffened when the catgirl receptionist looked at her, then glanced at Chris. "Are you aware of the charges filed against Ms. Sterkrou?"

Chris frowned. "I am not." He glanced at Kuro, who looked away, then looked back at the receptionist. "And I don't really care either. Kuro will tell me about them if she feels like it."

The look of gratitude Kuro sent Chris made him secure in his choice to not let whatever charges had been filed against her affect their relationship.

With a shrug, the receptionist typed on her

keyboard again. "That's fine. It is your choice, after all. And it's not like the charges against her affect your ability to make her your catpanion."

Once the woman had added them into her register, she asked them to sit tight and wait for the first person available to meet with them. All of them wandered over to the couch. Chris found himself surrounded on all sides by beautiful women. Silva was on his left. Kuro sat on his right. Elsa had decided to sit on the floor and place her head in his lap, which prompted him to stroke her beautiful blonde hair. The receptionist noticed this and cast him a wicked smile. Not the evil wicked smile, but the lewd wicked smile.

It caused his cheeks to turn red despite himself.

The wait wasn't long. Lily Sutor soon came out of the door behind the receptionist desk and locked eyes with him. He blushed harder when a smirk rose to her face, but he tried to ignore the knowing look she sent him as he and the catgirls stood up.

"I had a feeling this wouldn't be the last time I saw you," she said.

"You suspected I'd come in to register more catpanions?" Chris asked, furrowing his brow.

Lily Sutor nodded. "There are some humans who

naturally take to catgirls and their many eccentricities. Their adaptability, when confronted with something that goes against social norms, makes them great mates that catgirls are naturally drawn to. When I first saw you with Ms. Flint—I'm sorry, with Ms. Redford here—I knew your ability to accept the unusual traits and non-conforming nature catgirls are known for would lead to you entering a polyamorous relationship."

Chris wasn't sure how he felt about this woman suspecting he was going to enter a polyamorous relationship after one meeting, but he didn't think he could deny what she said. He had long ago accepted catgirls into his life. If he hadn't, he would never be able to change the way he viewed Elsa. He wouldn't have even considered it.

The process for filing Kuro and Elsa was a lot longer than the one for Silva. Part of that was because two catgirls were being registered instead of one, but another part of it was because three catgirls were now his catpanions. He had to file extra papers because he'd reached the point where his relationship was considered polyamorous.

"It looks like all the paperwork is in order," Lily said as she put the files he, Kuro, and Elsa had signed away. She then placed her hands on the desk and clasped them together as she looked at him. "Now, I should tell you that because you have three catpanions, the Catgirl Protection Bureau will require your financial records and information. You will also have to send them your tax files every year to make sure you're financially capable of supporting them. Of course, you can also file for financial aid through the government, but you have to show proof that you are working in order to have that financial aid. If it turns out you are eligible for financial aid, you'll have benefits such as tax reductions. That said, regardless of your financial situation, you may now expense your food to us. You'll need to send a copy of each receipt to the address listed in this brochure right here, and the Catgirl Protection Bureau will pay for your food." She paused to take a breath. "I highly recommend you read through that brochure. Many people haven't and come to regret it later when they find themselves in serious trouble, which could have been avoided if they had read it."

The amount of information this woman had for him was startling, but Chris took the brochure, which was titled *Catgirls and Polyamory*, and listened to everything she told him. He nodded several times when she finished.

"I understand," Chris said.

"Good. In that case, you four are done here." Lily smiled at them. "I hope you all enjoy your lives as a family unit."

chapter 2

THE WEEKEND PASSED with relative quickness after Kuro and Elsa registered as Chris's catpanions. They spent the rest of Saturday enjoying a day out, then Chris and Kuro traveled to Tanner's kickboxing center, where they sparred each other for several hours. Tanner had decided to let them be since Kuro had similar military training. Sunday was a lazy day. Kuro had gone back to Sister Ann's orphanage, while Chris, Elsa, and Silva spent the day watching television, playing video games, and snuggling on the couch.

Chris still hadn't slept with Elsa yet. He was doing his best to be good to her, but it was still hard to treat her differently from before. It took a conscious effort on his part to not treat her like a sibling.

Elsa, bless her heart, was understanding. Rather than getting annoyed by his slow pace, she did her best to help him by acting a bit more forward. She'd touch him intimately, kiss him on the cheek, and nuzzle her face against his chest. She hadn't kissed him on the lips yet, but Silva suspected Elsa was waiting for him to initiate that sort of intimacy—that was what she told Chris.

When Monday finally arrived, Chris was reluctant to leave the apartment, though he did indeed hop on the bus and make his way to school.

Two weeks had passed since he'd been to San Diego State University. It felt much longer thanks to everything that happened. As he walked to class, Chris watched as people walked by, frowned when a couple of stoners smelling of pot drifted across his vision and nose, and wondered how Professor Shinomiya and the others were doing.

He entered the classroom and went up to his usual spot, where he took a seat, got out his notebook, and prepared for the day. People trickled inside in ones and twos. It wasn't long before Anastasia appeared, noticed him, and grinned as she walked up to sit beside him.

"Finally off your suspension, I see," she said.

"Yeah, though now I kinda wish I was back on it." Chris grinned. "It was nice to finally take a break."

"I'll bet it was nice." Anastasia snorted. "What with the time you got to spend with that harem of catgirls you've gathered."

Chris winced, wondering if Anastasia knew about Kuro and Elsa, but he was sure she was just being sarcastic. They had registered. However, not only would it take time for the files to go through, but it wasn't like their relationship would be announced to the world. He took her words as more of a biting comment than one she said because she thought it was true.

"Are you still angry about… well, you know?" Chris asked.

Anastasia gave him a stare so blank Chris could only look away. While he was observing the pair of women two seats down, he heard a sigh from the blonde.

"No, I'm not angry about that anymore. I've had a long time to think about it, and honestly, I'm beginning to realize a relationship between us would have never worked out." Anastasia brought out her laptop, opened it, and booted it up. The screen flashed to her screensaver before she typed in her passcode, too fast for him to see. "You're a great guy. You're attractive, kind, helpful, and fun to be around, but you're the kind of person who'd help anyone if they needed it."

Chris wasn't so sure about that, but it was true that he had helped more than his fair share of people within the past few weeks. Silva, Kuro, Sister Ann, and the entire orphanage. If someone was in trouble, and he was present and knew he could help, he would probably do it.

Anastasia smiled as if she could see what he was thinking. "I don't want a man like that. I want a man who is nice, but I don't want that kindness to extend to others. I want to be the most important thing in his world. That's something I don't think you can give me. The more I realized that, the less angry I felt."

"Well, you do have a point there. I probably couldn't like that for you, or for anyone, if I'm being honest." Chris ran a hand through his hair. "So, then, what does that make us now? Friends? Classmates?"

Her nose scrunching up in a cute gesture, Anastasia thought about his question for a moment, then smiled and said, "I think friends is a good word to describe our relationship."

"Then I'm glad we're friends." Chris smiled. "Also, as your friend, remember that you can always come to me if you need help."

"I know I can," Anastasia said, also smiling.

At that moment, Professor Shinomiya came in. As usual, she placed her water bottle and purse on the desk. Her eyes scanned the crowd before locking onto Chris.

"Glad to have you back with us, Mr. Redford," she said.

"It's good to be back, Professor," Chris responded.

Professor Shinomiya smiled, but it wasn't a kind smile, though he wouldn't call it vicious either. It was more of a mischievous smile, something the professor didn't wear very often. Whatever the reason, seeing that look sent a chill down his spine.

He found out why seconds later.

"You say that now, but you missed an important test last week on the differences between human and catgirl anatomy… which I will expect you to make up today. Your task will be to write up a five-page, double-spaced essay centered around one specific organ. Your objective will be to share the differences and similarities between a catgirl's organ and a human one. You'll need to hand it in to me before I leave at… 5 pm."

As he heard Professor Shinomiya's words, Chris could do nothing except groan.

***

Silva stared at her phone with a frown. On it was a simple message. *I'll be home late tonight.* It was from Chris, of course, which was the reason for her frown. She didn't know why he was going to be late, though she assumed it had something to do with school, and she wanted a bit more context.

"Nya ha ha! What's wrong, Silva?" asked Elsa as she sat on the couch, staring at her laptop.

"Chris is going to be late," Silva said with a sigh. She sat down next to Elsa and looked at what the other catgirl was looking at. "Is that the GoFundMe for Sister Ann?"

"Nya ha ha ha! It is indeed."

"The number has risen."

Silva was right. The amount of money the fundraiser had earned last time had been about $250,000 or so, but the number had gone up to $300,000. Having never dealt with money until recently, Silva could hardly fathom how much that was. She only knew it was a lot.

"The fundraiser ended just last night, so they won't be making any more." Sitting with her legs crossed, Elsa crossed her arms and stared at the number. "Of course, it's not like they need any more money. With that kind of cash, they can pay off their debt and afford to remodel the entire orphanage. Well, maybe. I suppose it would depend on the remodeling. At the very least, they should be able to afford some nicer furniture."

Silva smiled as she thought about how the kids

and her fellow catgirls were now safe from danger and would be able to live more comfortably. She was glad she had played a part in that, however small it might have been. Doing something good for others also made her wonder if this was why Chris helped so many people. She shook her head. Probably not. He didn't even seem to think about stuff like this when he helped others.

"So then…" Elsa suddenly whipped out her PSP from who knows where and grinned at Silva. "Want to hunt some monsters with me?"

"Sure," Silva said with a giggle.

The two of them spent several hours playing *Monster Hunter* for the PSP. Silva was not very good. She truthfully didn't much care for video games, but she knew Elsa and Chris loved them, and she wanted to understand what they liked so much. It was her hope that she could gain this understanding by playing with them.

At some point, while she and Elsa were playing, Kuro arrived and joined them. She didn't play, of course, but she told them all about how the other catgirls were doing at the orphanage while Silva made them lunch. It turned out Sister Ann had paid off her debt before the deadline and was in the process of buying better furniture and supplies.

"She wants to remodel, but we don't have enough money for that," Kuro said. "That's why Sister Ann decided to buy other items like better beds, tables, chairs, and some toys the kids can play with. She's even planning to buy a large screen TV so everyone can watch movies."

"Nya ha ha! Sounds like things are looking up," Elsa said as Silva came out carrying a plate of sandwiches. They were simple, made from a variety of deli meats, cheese, lettuce, and vegetables.

Kuro scarfed them down with zeal.

The hours passed by. The time when Chris would normally arrive home passed, and Silva realized she could no longer hold off on making dinner. Kuro was getting hungry and Elsa's stomach was rumbling. But when she looked at the fridge, she realized they didn't have enough food to make anything.

"It looks I need to head to the grocery store," Silva told them.

"I'll go with you," Kuro said as she stood up from the couch. Elsa was still playing her PSP, though it sounded like she was playing something aside from *Monster Hunter*.

"Thanks." Silva gave her friend and fellow catpanion a smile. "I'm… still not very fond of going outside by myself."

"I'm always here for you," Kuro said with a shrug and a smile of her own.

The grocery store where Chris shopped was called Sprouts Farmers Market, and it was just an eighteen-minute walk to reach. With Kuro keeping her company, Silva had no trouble reaching the store and doing her grocery shopping in just a little under an hour. Before long, Kuro and Silva were walking out of the grocery store, several bags in hand.

Silva looked up at the sky. The sun was going down. Clouds were painted in vibrant hues of pink and red, which caused it to look like fire was stretching across the sky. A slight breeze blew through the street, causing Silva to shiver despite wearing long sleeves. As they began walking back home, Kuro raised the bags in her hand.

"What exactly are you planning to make with this?" she asked.

"I want to make southern Indian fish curry," Silva explained. "I saw a recipe for it a little while ago and thought it would be nice to try out."

"You've really become quite the cook," Kuro said, looking happy. "I'm glad you were able to find something you—"

She stopped talking, her face stiffening. The sudden and abrupt silence caused Silva to look up.

"Kuro?" she questioned.

Kuro leaned in close, putting her arm around Silva's shoulder as they kept walking. A moment later, the much larger catgirl's warm breath was washing over her ear. However warm her fellow catpanion's breath was, the words Kuro said left her feeling cold.

"Keep walking. Act like nothing is wrong." She paused. "We're being followed."

"W-what?"

It took everything Silva had not to look around. She wanted to glance all over, to find whoever was following them, but she knew it wouldn't be a good idea. Kuro had told her not to respond because she didn't want the person or people following them to know they knew they were being followed.

"Who's following us?" she asked.

"I'm not sure, but they're driving a beat-up Cadillac." Kuro's eyes darted toward something, a window. "You can see the car if you look in that window."

Silva followed Kuro's gaze and looked in the window, where she did indeed find a Cadillac driving down the road at a pace far slower than the speed limit. The windows were tinted. She couldn't see whoever was inside of them. They could have been anyone, and just because they were going slower than the speed limit didn't mean they were following her and Kuro. But Silva realized with a growing sense of trepidation that there was almost no one on this street aside from them, and as they turned a corner, so too did the car.

Her heartbeat quickened.

"What… should we do?" asked Silva.

"On my lead, we break into a run," Kuro said. "We're not going back home yet. Just follow me."

"O-okay."

Silva tried to steady her breathing as Kuro pulled back, only to grab her by the hand. Kuro's much larger hand wrapped around hers would have normally been comforting. Not right now. Her heart was thundering in her chest. It felt like something was trying to beat its way out of her ribcage. Every fiber in her body felt like electricity was coursing through it, and not the good kind she felt when she and Chris were having sex.

"On three," Kuro said. "One. Two. Three. Now!"

At Kuro's shout, Silva broke into a run with Kuro, though it was more like she was being dragged behind the larger catgirl, who ran so fast there was no way Silva could have kept up. Her breathing quickly became ragged as buildings and walls passed by in a blur. Kuro had already led her off the path she took with Chris, so she had no idea where they were anymore.

Despite knowing it was a bad idea, Silva looked behind them and saw the car had picked up speed. It was now gaining on them. Kuro managed to keep ahead by racing through several alleys, which were too small for the car to travel through, but then the men who'd been inside got out and began chasing them on foot. There were eight of them. A shudder of fear ran through Silva's body when she noticed how all of the men were carrying guns and wearing masks.

"Down this way!" Kuro shouted as she raced into another alley. This one was filled with trash cans. Kuro moved several trash cans out of the way, then pushed Silva between them.

The smell was rancid. Silva's nose wrinkled. It was like something had died inside of these trash cans and been left to rot, but she didn't complain. Not a single peep left her mouth.

The look in Kuro's eyes kept her from saying anything.

"Stay here," Kuro commanded before running back out of the alley.

Silva watched her go, shivering as she wondered what she should do, but then she realized there was nothing she could do. Whoever these people were, whatever they wanted, it was not something Silva had the strength to deal with, which meant staying put as

Kuro told her to was all she was capable of. As this realization sank in, Silva sank to the cold cement. She hugged her knees to her chest and buried her face between them, shivering.

"Chris…" she muttered as if calling his name would summon him to her.

But of course, it didn't. All that appeared was a cold breeze that sent an ominous whistle echoing through the alley.

***

Kuro had made sure the men caught sight of her before running off. Her feet pounded on the pavement, her breathing was harsh in her ears, and her heart was thudding against her ribcage, threatening to break free. She felt adrenaline race through her veins. Rather than fear, what Kuro felt was excitement. A euphoria that she hadn't felt since her time in the military.

"There she is!"

"Don't let her get away!"

"Quick! Catch that fucking bitch!"

Glancing over her shoulder, Kuro saw the men chasing them. There were seven in total. She frowned for a moment, having thought there were eight, but then she shrugged and kept going. Leading this group away from Silva, Kuro didn't stop running until she had reached an alley that would give her an advantage over their numbers.

Of course, this alley ended in a dead-end.

"Nowhere to run now, you cunt," one of the men said.

It was hard to judge these men by their appearance. They wore pants and long-sleeved shirts, face masks around their mouths to hide their features, and caps or hoodies to further mask the color of their hair. The only thing about them she noticed were the guns. Having spent enough time in the military, she knew what kind of guns these were. They were a mix of weapons. She saw everything from the Beretta PX4 Semi-automatic to the Browning 1911-380. Fortunately, there were no rifles or automatic weapons among them, or she would have actually been in trouble.

The men approached her slowly.

"Is this really the catgirl we're after?" asked one of them. "She's kinda… big."

Kuro twitched at being called big, but it wasn't like they were wrong. She towered over every man present. In fact, most of these men were even shorter than Chris, who stood at a respectable six feet, making her look even larger to them.

"You boys need something from me?" Kuro asked, feigning nonchalance.

While it was impossible to tell what sort of expression they were making, Kuro had a feeling the one in front was frowning.

"We need you to come with us," he said, pointing his gun at her. "Don't make this difficult. Just follow us and we won't fucking shoot you."

So they needed her, and probably Silva too, which meant this wasn't a random attack. They were after her and Silva for a reason. That was good to know, but she shoved the knowledge aside for now. First things first, she had to get out of this situation.

"I'm afraid I'll have to decline," Kuro said with a fanged grin.

Before the lead man could even pull the trigger, Kuro had moved into his guard with a single step. She grabbed the outstretched arm holding the gun. With a quick tug, she had jerked the man into her waiting knee. A loud retching sound echoed around the alley as the man doubled over her knee, the air leaving his lungs, bile spewing to the ground.

"Shit! Fire!"

The others panicked and shot at her, heedless of the fact that their leader was still in the line of fire. Their bullets penetrated the man's back and head.

Blood spewed from new holes forming on his skin. His body jerked and twitched with each bullet that hit him, though most went wide and struck a wall or the floor. Finally, the sound of guns clicking empty reached their ears, causing them to pale.

Kuro was no longer there.

She had used her superior strength to leap onto the wall and, in complete defiance of gravity, ran along the vertical surface to escape their gunfire. Once she heard their guns click empty, the muscles in her thighs flexed as she shoved off the wall, which cracked beneath her feet.

Landing with a thud, Kuro bent her knees and placed her left hand on the ground. A second later, she was sweeping out her right leg in a low kick that caught one of her attackers by the ankle. He screamed and went down, which alerted the others to the fact that she was among them.

Placing both hands on the ground, Kuro used the incredible strength in her muscles to lift her lower body, then slammed a mule kick into the falling man's chest. A loud *crack* like thunder echoing nearby was followed by the man's agonized screaming as he flew through the air. The screams were cut off, however, when he struck a wall before hitting the ground with a thump.

"What the fuck is going on here?!"

"Is this bitch some kind of super woman?!"

Kuro grinned at being called a super woman, and she thanked the man for his compliment by poking out his eyes with her fingers. He screamed, dropped his gun, and reached for his eyes. She rabbit-punched him in the throat.

While he was gagging, she pulled him into a punch meant for her. He took the hit right in the face and crumbled like a sack of bricks. The man who attacked him stared at his own fist in surprise, then Kuro put him down with a rising high kick that slammed into his temple. He was going to wake up with a massive concussion.

There were only three left. All of them looked shocked and frightened by what they had just witnessed, their bodies trembling like leaves caught in a storm as their eyes widened and the blood drained from their faces. They didn't even think to reload their guns. Kuro was sure they would have run away, except now she was the one blocking the entrance.

"You people made a huge mistake when you came after me," she said, grinning from ear to ear as she stalked forward like a predator in the savanna. "Now you're going to pay for that mistake."

Just before Kuro was prepared to take the

remaining three down, a voice came from behind her.

"Don't fucking move or this bitch is gonna get her brains blown out!"

Kuro looked over her shoulder, a vicious glare on her face, but that expression froze at what she saw. A man, the eighth man she believed she had imagined, was standing at the entrance of the alley, and he had Silva in his grip. Her fellow catgirl was frightened. Her eyes were wide, face paler than normal. Pointed at her temple was a gun. It was a Taurus Millennium G2 Pistol. It wasn't a great weapon, and in fact wasn't even that good in her mind, but it would still put a bullet through Silva's head if he pulled the trigger.

She gritted her teeth and gave the man her most hateful look. Even with that mask covering his face, she could sense the arrogance pouring from him. She imagined he was grinning beneath that mask.

"That's right. I've got this pretty little bitch, and if you don't want her brains being splattered all over this alley, I suggest you do as I say."

"K-Kuro..." Silva muttered, then she yelped when the man tugged on her hair.

"What do you want me to do?" Kuro gritted her teeth.

"Get down on your knees," the man ordered.

Kuro didn't want to do anything this man said,

but with Silva's life hanging in the balance, she really had no choice. She got down on her knees. The cold pavement jolted her skin, but she ignored it and kept her gaze locked on the man.

"Tie her up," the man said with a gesture at the remaining three thugs.

They moved forward, producing a rope from somewhere. As they reached her and began tying her up, Kuro's eyes locked with Silva, who was shivering but had an oddly determined expression on her face. She didn't know what that meant, didn't know what the silver-haired catgirl was thinking. Whatever it was, she did not expect what happened next.

In a surprising burst of speed, Silva grabbed the man's gun arm, pulled it down, and sank her teeth into his forearm. Blood welled up on his arm as her teeth easily broke his skin. A loud scream of surprise and pain escaped the man's mouth. He dropped the gun, which clattered to the floor.

"You fucking cunt!"

Yanking his arm from her mouth, the man backhanded Silva. She screamed as she was sent to the floor. Holding a hand to her cheek, she looked up as the man she'd bitten went down on her, pinning her to the ground.

"That fucking does it! You wanna fuck with me?!

Fine! Then I'm gonna fuck with you! I'll fuck you up real good!"

Before he could do much more than scream those words, Kuro acted. She broke the ropes they had tried to bind her with, grabbed the heads of two of the three thugs between her large hands, and slammed their heads together.

The loud cracking noise as their skulls fractured was enough to distract the man on top of Silva. With a hiss, she clawed at his face, eliciting another pained yell. During that time, Kuro finished off the last one with a heavy reverse heel kick to the ribs. As the man went down, frothing at the mouth, she raced toward the thug straddling Silva, screaming his eyes out as he held a hand over his bleeding face. His scream was abruptly cut off when she punted him in the head like she was kicking a football for a field goal. He flew off Silva, struck the ground, skidded for several feet, and stopped.

He didn't get back up.

Kuro waited for a moment to see if there were any more enemies, but all that remained were the people moaning and groaning on the ground. She knelt beside Silva and held out a hand.

"Are you okay?" she asked.

"I... I'm..." Silva stared at the hand, then at Kuro's face as tears welled up in her eyes. She only had a second to realize what was going to happen before Silva lunged forward and buried her face into Kuro's chest, crying her eyes out. "I was so scared! That man grabbed me and pointed a gun at me! He told me to shut up or he was going to kill me! And then... and then... he—!"

"Shh." Kuro began running a hand over Silva's head, calming the girl down. "It's okay. Everything is okay now."

While Silva did cry for a bit, she proved how much stronger she'd become mentally by stopping after only a few minutes. Pulling away, she rubbed her eyes, drying them of tears before looking at Kuro with a determined expression.

"We need to call the police," she said.

Kuro nodded. "We should also call Chris."

"Yes." Silva agreed.

Kuro took one last look at the men lying on the ground around her as Silva pulled out her smartphone and dialed 911. She furrowed her brow. Someone had come after her and Silva. She didn't know who or for what purpose, but she had every intention of finding out.

chapter 3

CHRIS WAS NEARLY OUT of breath when he arrived at the scene of the crime. It was already late at night, the sky was dark, the stars were out, and the flashing of several police cars and ambulances stood out starkly against the backdrop of the black roads. With fear racing through his heart, he made for the scene.

As he approached, it didn't take long to spot Kuro and Silva. Kuro was standing tall with her back straight and shoulders squared as a pair of police officers with the emblem of the Catgirl Protection Bureau questioned her. Burrowed into her side was Silva. The smaller catgirl looked shaken, but even so, she still spoke when they questioned her.

"Halt!" a voice suddenly shouted, forcing Chris to stop. He turned as a police officer walked over to him. "This area is currently restricted to civilians. I'm going to have to ask you to leave."

Chris frowned, though he didn't get angry at this officer for just doing his job. He didn't know that Chris was indirectly involved.

Getting ready to show his identification to this officer, Chris was not given the chance because Silva spotted him moments before he could explain his circumstances.

"Chris!"

The girl bolted away from Kuro's side, raced toward him, and flung her arms around his neck. Her crying as she buried her face in his neck sent sharp pain through his chest. She had suffered from something terrible, and he hadn't been there to help. Even though he knew, logically, that there was nothing he could have done, it still didn't make Chris feel better.

"I'm sorry I wasn't there to protect you," Chris said as he stroked her hair. Silva's cat ears twitched when he rubbed them.

Back where Silva had been standing, Kuro and the two officers stared at them, perhaps out of surprise that he had arrived. However, Kuro's eyes lit up as she turned to the police and said something. They nodded their heads. As a group, they turned in his direction and made their way over to him.

"At ease, Officer," one of them said. She placed a hand on the shoulder of the police officer who'd stopped him. "These two catgirls are this man's catpanions. We'll take it from here."

The police officer, who looked quite young and eager, frowned but gave the woman a swift salute. In the darkness of the night, Chris gazed at the female police officer. She had dark skin and dark hair. Her eyes were a warm brown. It took him a moment, but she soon recognized her, as well as the redhead by her side.

"Officer Hudson. Officer Demire. It seems we have been meeting quite often these days."

The two officers gave him wide grins that were both amused and resigned.

"You seem to be caught in the middle of more trouble," Officer Hudson said.

"Is it okay if I know what happened here?" Chris asked. "All I got was a text from Silva saying she and Kuro were attacked, but I don't know the exact details."

"They were attacked by a gang called the Acre Boys," Officer Hudson said. "They're a fairly well-known gang who bases themselves in Lincoln Acres. They are best known for their hate crimes, theft, and drug dealings. We had troubles with them in the past, but they quieted down after we managed to arrest most of their members. I'm a little surprised they suddenly became active again, and they tried to kidnap two catgirls, which is a criminal offense that can earn a life sentence in prison."

As he listened to what they were telling him, Chris found himself frowning. He placed his hands around Silva's waist, running his hand along her smooth back, which caused the catgirl to begin purring as she calmed down. After casting a glance at Kuro to make sure she was okay, he looked back at Officers Hudson and Demire.

"Why would a gang based out of Lincoln Acres come all the way here to kidnap two catgirls?"

"That's the question, isn't it?" Officer Hudson shrugged. "Your catpanion here seems to think they were hired to do it. I'm personally inclined to believe her. Even the Acre Boys wouldn't be stupid enough to try kidnapping a couple of catgirls unless they were being handsomely paid for their services."

"So someone put them up to this?" asked Chris.

"So we think. We can't know for sure until we question them, but..."

"But?" Chris asked when Officer Hudson trailed off.

"But they won't be talking for a while," Officer Hudson finished with a resigned smile. "Your catpanion here is quite vicious. Most of the gang members have either broken ribs or cracked skulls. We won't be able to question them until their injuries are healed, which could take a few weeks or maybe even a month depending on the extent of their injuries."

Chris glanced at Kuro, who saw his look, complete with raised eyebrow. She blushed and looked away. Even so, there was an incredibly stubborn look on her face, the kind of look that said, *"Don't look at me. This isn't my fault."*

He sighed, then looked back at the two officers.

"If someone did put them up to this, won't not being able to question them put us in more jeopardy? Who's to say whoever did this won't just hire another gang to come after us?" asked Chris.

"You bring up a good point, but there's really nothing we can do," Officer Hudson said with a head shake. "Even we have rules and protocols we must abide by."

He wanted to complain, even though he knew it wouldn't accomplish anything. Someone had attacked Kuro and Silva, and they would probably continue hiring people to come after them so long as the attacks were not tracked back to them. The very thought cast a red haze over his mind. If he thought he had the ability to do so, he would have gone after whoever had hired this gang himself.

As he thought about gangs, Chris remembered something important.

"Do you think this attack could somehow be related to the shooting at the restaurant we were at last week?" asked Chris.

"Shooting?" Officer Hudson looked confused.

"Oh! I remember hearing about that," Officer Demire suddenly said, causing her partner to turn and look at her. "Chris and his catpanions were eating at a Korean restaurant when a drive-by shooting occurred. It was filed as a random act of violence." The redhead paused to look at him with a concentrated frown. "You believe it wasn't random?"

"I wasn't sure at first, but I've always had the sense that someone had hired them to do it," Chris said, paused, then sighed. "I can't say if these events are related or not, but last week, I began helping a sister who runs an orphanage. She had taken out a loan from a loan shark named Calvin Lafaard. A little while after I agreed to help her, Lafaard 'coincidentally' bumped into me when I was shopping for groceries with Silva. He tried to pay me off so I wouldn't help Sister Ann, and when I refused, he said he hoped I 'wouldn't regret' my choice… for Silva's sake."

Officers Hudson and Demire glanced at each other. Chris could almost see the gears turning in their heads. Neither he, Silva, nor Kuro said anything, and so the silence stretched on until both officers looked back at him.

"We have had issues with Calvin Lafaard before," Officer Hudson admitted at last. "He's been charged several times with fraudulent activity, but none of the charges ever stuck. He uses legal loopholes to avoid being convicted. However, he's well-known for being petty and vindictive. Several of his business rivals were convicted of multiple crimes and put out of business, but a lot of us at the police department believe the evidence we found was planted to throw us off his trail."

"So you think this could be Lafaard's doing?" asked Kuro.

"I do." Officer Hudson nodded.

"What can we do about this?" asked Chris.

"I'll pull up the report you filed on the drive-by shooting," Officer Hudson explain to him. "If possible, I'd like to find the people who did it and question them. We'll also question the people who attacked Kuro and Silva tonight, once they are well enough to answer our questions. Until then, I'm going to increase police patrols of this area. Lafaard is a cautious man, which is how he's been able to avoid being convicted of any crimes. He won't do anything once the police get involved."

Chris wasn't sure he liked the idea since it meant

they couldn't do anything proactive to take this guy down, but he also understood there really was nothing they could do. He accepted this.

Kuro and Silva were asked a few more questions, but most of the questioning was already complete. The police let them go a little while later. They walked home under cover of darkness, the cool night air causing Silva to shiver as she leaned into him. Kuro did not, but he expected that. As he glanced at the tall woman walking beside him, a frown marred his face.

"What is it?" asked Kuro.

"Are you okay?" he asked.

"What do you mean? Can't you see I'm perfectly fine?" Kuro thrust a thumb at herself and showed off her fangs by fiercely grinning at him. "There is no way a couple of half-assed thugs would be able to hurt me."

"I know you're perfectly capable of taking care of yourself, but that doesn't stop me from worrying," Chris admitted.

Kuro looked away. "W-well, ahem, I do appreciate your concern, but I'm perfectly all right."

Chris accepted her words with a nod. They finished walking through Memorial Park, entered their apartment complex, and made it to their apartment. Elsa was still there, playing *Monster Hunter World* on the Xbox One. It looked like she hadn't left that couch all day.

"You guys are back," she exclaimed. "Nya ha ha! Took you long enough—is something the matter? What's with the somber expressions?"

"I'll leave Kuro to explain what happened," Chris said before turning to Silva. "Do you want to make dinner with me, or should I cook?"

Silva had been glued to his side ever since he showed up at the crime scene. She looked at him with her big, heterochromatic eyes, head tilted slightly to the left. A moment passed before she nodded.

"I would like to cook with you," she said, then paused. "But we don't have any food… and the food we bought for dinner tonight has spoiled."

Chris hadn't realized that, but now that he was thinking about it, he remembered they hadn't had time to do any grocery shopping. That must have been why Silva and Kuro were out so late. With a sigh, he thought about what they should do for dinner.

"I guess we'll be ordering pizza then," he said.

While Chris ordered a pizza, Kuro sat down next to Elsa and explained what happened to her and Silva. Elsa's response was surprisingly ferocious. Her eyes narrowed into slits as she hissed in anger. Then she expressed her sorrow that she hadn't been around to help Kuro and Silva out, though Kuro said it was better that she hadn't been there.

Their pizza arrived half an hour later. It was pretty late at night, around 9 pm, but the group sat around the dinner table and ate anyway. Silva seemed to perk up a little as she munched on the pizza. He learned that she'd never actually eaten pizza before because her Grams didn't like her eating junk food, so this was something of a treat for her.

After dinner, Chris headed into the bathroom to take a shower. He hadn't done so today since he'd rushed out of the kickboxing center the moment he got Silva's message. His body was covered in dried sweat. He was pretty sure he smelled rancid.

As he rinsed off his body, the door to the bathroom suddenly opened and Kuro walked inside. She wasn't wearing any clothes, though she did have a towel around her waist, keeping her modesty barely intact. Her massive breasts strained against the fabric. Likewise, her muscular hips and thighs flexed as she closed the door and walked toward him.

"I've decided to take a shower with you. Hope you don't mind," she said.

"I don't think there is a single man in the entire world who would mind if you joined him in the shower," Chris admitted with a chuckle. "Come on in."

Kuro flashed him a fanged grin. "That's the kind

of answer I like to hear."

Kuro removed the towel from around her waist, massive breasts jiggling. Chris eyed her tits as they hung off her frame like a pair of water balloons filled to the point where they might burst. Her dark brown nipples were a shade darker than her skin, her areolae a shade lighter than her nipples. He glanced down further at her trim pussy. There was just a small patch of hair present, but it was clear she took care of herself down there.

"Enjoying the view?" asked Kuro as she stepped into the shower. Now that she was so close, her breasts were practically in his face. As if to present them even more, Kuro leaned over, placed her hands on the wall, and grinned down at him, her tits swinging back and forth like pendulums. It was hypnotic.

"Of course. This is a sight I could never grow tired of," Chris said.

"You can do more than just admire them, though," Kuro offered.

It was an offer that Chris had no trouble taking. He reached out and hefted her tits in his hand. They were surprisingly heavy. He didn't know how such a muscular woman who had so little body fat could have such incredible breasts, but he would be lying if he said he wasn't impressed, especially since he could tell from their feel that they were all-natural.

Kuro's breathing picked up as Chris ran his index fingers over her nipples, moving them in circles around her areolae before flicking her nipples back and forth. Almost fascinated by what he was seeing, Chris poked a finger into her breasts and watched in awe as his finger literally sank into her skin. Soft and springy, her breasts were probably the most incredible examples of womanhood he'd ever seen.

"Are you… just going to stand there… p-poking them?" asked Kuro.

"No, I'm not. Forgive me." Chris chuckled as he grabbed a handful of her left tit. "I was so in awe of them I nearly forgot myself."

"It's okay—hnnn!"

Kuro released a strained gasp as Chris leaned down and sucked her nipple into his mouth. It quickly hardened as he swirled his tongue around it, flicking it back and forth, then taking it between his teeth and giving it a good tug. She seemed to enjoy that. The groan she produced when he tugged on her nipple was far louder than anything else she'd released.

It wasn't long before playing with her nipples wasn't enough; he leaned down and began kissing her stomach. He let his lips graze against her abs, which were harder and more durable than his own, an incredible six-pack that he'd only seen a few bodybuilders possess. This perfectly sculpted stomach left him breathless, and he couldn't stop himself from kissing and trailing his tongue across it.

"Ha… ha… mrrrr…"

Kuro released an odd noise that sounded like it was half purr and half moan. When he glanced up, he saw her looking at him with hooded eyes filled with desire. The wanton lust visible inside of them made his dick twitch.

Finally kneeling on his haunches, Chris reached the treasure. Kuro's pussy. He gazed at her soft outer lips as he let his hand trail along the outside. Kuro's thighs clenched as he brushed against her skin with feather-light touches, then stiffened more when he spread her lips apart with two fingers. Her insides were wet, but he was sure that was the shower and steam. Leaning forward, he stuck out his tongue and gave her a long, thorough lick.

Her taste intoxicated him.

"A-are you just going to keep teasing me?!" demanded Kuro as Chris lapped at her pussy but didn't do anything more. "Damn it, Chris! I did not come here for this light foreplay! If you aren't going to fuck me with that tongue, then I'm gonna—"

Her words were interrupted by a loud moan as

Chris pressed his mouth against her pussy and penetrated her folds with his tongue. She clenched her teeth as his tongue wiggled around inside of her. When his tongue suddenly curled and rubbed against an area of her vaginal walls that was harder than the rest, her legs and body shook as she arched her back and released a louder than normal moan. The loud *"Hhrrrrrn!!"* she let out was husky and deep. Kuro had the kind of smoky voice that could drive a man insane.

Once she was good and wet, Chris leaned back and pushed two fingers into her vagina, causing Kuro to release a loud but strained groan. He began pumping. In and out. As he did, he worked her clit out from underneath its hood, then placed his mouth over it and began furiously rubbing the small bundle of nerves with his tongue.

"Hyk! Heee! Haa! Haaa! Purr!"

Kuro began panting, moaning, and purring as he ate her out. Her juices flowed around his fingers and mouth, dripping down her quivering thighs. She leaned over further as her legs buckled like she was going to fall. She didn't, though, perhaps because she didn't want him to see her in a moment of weakness even while they were doing foreplay. It was not too much longer that her pussy began twitching, and then she was cumming into his mouth, and Chris lapped up her juices.

"Ha… ha…"

With her eyes closed, Kuro breathed deeply several times, her chest and shoulders heaving with every inhale and exhale. There was a pleased smile on her face. When she opened her eyes and gazed down at him, Chris spotted her fangs glinting in the light as she peeled her lips back into a grin.

"It's too bad this shower is so small," she complained. "If it was bigger, me and you could do a lot more than just this."

Chris wanted to say that it wasn't because the bath was small but because she was so large, but he didn't. She had a point anyway. This bathtub wasn't the biggest. Even Chris would not lounge in this tub with his six feet of height. How could Kuro, who stood at somewhere around seven feet, possibly be able to have sex in such a small space? Even straddling his waist would be a problem.

"It does suck," Chris agreed. "But I can at least wash you off."

"Please do," Kuro said, her grin changing into a smile.

Chris helped wash Kuro's body with soap. He couldn't shampoo her hair because she was so much taller than him, but he left that part to her. She used the detachable shower head to her advantage as she washed her hair. When she was finished, Kuro helped him clean his front, which was covered in her juices and his sweat. Then they both climbed out of the shower and dried off.

It was at this time that Kuro finally discovered the joys of having someone dry and comb her hair.

"This is nice." She closed her eyes as she sat on a small stool. Chris was behind her. As he looked at them in the mirror, an amused smile appeared on his face, though Kuro didn't notice since her eyes were still closed. "I remember Silva telling me about your talent for drying and combing a woman's hair." She chuckled. "I didn't believe it until now."

"I've had a lot of practice," Chris said as he used a blow dryer to dry off her hair and a specially made comb for catgirls to get the knots out.

"How is Silva?" he asked.

"She's fine." Kuro paused. "She fell asleep before I came in here. I wouldn't have left her side if she hadn't already fallen asleep. Elsa is asleep too."

Chris nodded. "Sorry I wasn't there to help out."

"Even if you had been there, you couldn't have done anything." Kuro grinned. "I had the whole situation under control. All you'd have been able to do was watch in awe as I kicked ass."

"You bring up a good point," Chris said. "Even now I haven't won a single one of our spars… and I'm pretty sure you go easy on me."

Kuro shrugged. "Military hand-to-hand combat is all about efficiently killing your enemy before they kill you. If I used the combat I learned during training in a simple spar, it could result in serious injury or death."

Chris knew quite a bit about the military and their training thanks to Tanner, who taught him a non-lethal version of what the military taught. The man had told him a lot of things. Of course, he refused to talk about his missions or some of the more gruesome aspects that came from being in the military, like what happened during his time in Iraq. Still, what Chris did know was enough to give him a general idea of the power someone with military training possessed.

After Kuro's hair was dry, the two made their way into the bedroom. Elsa and Silva were indeed asleep already. The two were cuddled together like a pair of adorable kittens… except they were way too hot to be just kittens. Silva was sleeping with her head resting on Elsa's boobs. Her pajama shirt was riding up, revealing her creamy white stomach. Elsa's shirt was unbuttoned, which meant the valley of her breasts were laid bare before his eyes, and considering the

sheer mass of her mountains, there was a lot of valley.

"I don't think it will be long before I stop seeing her as a simple family member," Chris muttered. He'd said that mostly to himself, but Kuro heard him and snorted to contain her laughter.

"Come on, perv. Let's get in bed," she said.

Chris nodded as he put on his boxers while Kuro pulled a pair of panties up her hips. She didn't wear anything else. Climbing into bed, she held up the covers, a clear invitation that Chris was more than happy to take. He climbed into bed and found Kuro pulling him close. It was odd being the person on top. It was normally the other way around, with the girl lying on top of the guy as she used his shoulder or chest as a pillow, but Chris wasn't one for conventional semantics like that. Kuro's soft and large tits made great pillows.

With a sigh of content, Chris closed his eyes and drifted off.

****

The next few weeks continued as usual. Chris went to school, studied, went to the kickboxing center, then came home to find Silva cooking dinner, Kuro setting the table, and Elsa playing video games or doing marketing promotions for his mother's company on her laptop. Nothing had really changed except the increased number of police cars that patrolled the streets every day.

Because of what happened, Kuro had become Silva's dedicated bodyguard. Whenever the silver-haired catgirl went out while Chris was at school, she would go with her. None of them knew if such an action was needed. However, all of them felt better knowing Kuro was around to protect them. She was easily the strongest and most skilled combatant out of them all, so her presence was reassuring.

Like that, one month passed without incident.

***

Chris wove back and forth as he dodged Tanner's strikes. The man launched several powerful and swift jabs that came so close to hitting him that he could feel the air pressure slamming him in the face. He shuffled back, avoided another attack, then tried to launch a counter, though it was swiftly blocked.

"All right. I think that's enough," Tanner commented with a smile. His body was covered in sweat and he was breathing heavier than usual. "Good job today."

"Thanks, Captain," Chris said, shoulders and chest heaving. He grabbed a towel hanging from the ring and used it to wipe the sweat off his face and armpits.

"How are things at home?" asked Tanner.

"Quiet," Chris said. "Nothing's happened since the attack. I don't know if that means Lafaard has decided to give up, or if he's just laying low until the police decide it's not worth sending out more patrols."

Tanner crossed his arms as he leaned against the boxing ring. "That's got you worried, huh?"

"I'd be lying if I said it didn't." Chris signed and ran a hand through his sweaty hair.

"Well, try not to worry too much. Worrying never helped anyone. Instead, just keep your eyes peeled for any unusual activity," Tanner said.

Chris nodded. "I will."

He spoke with Tanner for a little bit longer before heading to the showers. He went up to his locker and pulled out his gym bag. As he was removing his towel, his smartphone dropped to the floor with a clatter. He went to pick it up, then saw the screen and realized he had a missed call. It was from the police.

Thanks to what happened, Chris had the personal desk numbers of Officers Hudson and Demire in case of an emergency. Since Officer Hudson was the one who had called him, he selected her contact info, hit the call button, and listened as ringing filled his ear.

"Hello?" a voice said from the other end. It was Officer Hudson.

"Officer Hudson? It's me, Chris."

"Oh, Chris! I'm guessing you got my message?"

"Um, no. I just saw that you'd called and thought something had happened, so I called back."

"I see. Well, in that case, I'll tell you about what happened." There was a pause from the other end. Chris held his breath. *"We've questioned all the people who attacked Kuro and Silva. Sadly, they didn't have any information for us. It seems whoever hired them did so through an intermediary, a middle-man. What's more, the man who they said they talked to has disappeared, and we haven't been able to track them down."*

"That... sucks," Chris said. It was all he could think to say. Did this mean their investigation had hit a dead end?

"But I've got good news," Officer Hudson continued. *"I pulled up that report of the drive-by shooting you were caught in and managed to track down the license and registration of the truck those people were driving. It belonged to one of the people who was involved in that incident. It was another gang*

called Fifth Blood. They're based close to the restaurant you were at when the drive-by happened. After questioning them, we discovered they had also been hired by someone to shoot at you. Fortunately, this person hadn't gone into hiding, or maybe he had and re-emerged after deeming it safe. Either way, we now have him in custody and were able to interrogate him. Guess what we learned?"

As the woman continued to speak, Chris felt excitement bubbling in his chest. It sounded like they had managed to find a lead. As she finished her dialogue with a question, Chris could hardly contain himself as he answered.

"You discovered a lead to Calvin Lafaard?" he asked.

"Bingo. We don't have enough to convict him right now, but we do have enough to write up a search warrant for his house and all of his property. We've already got several squads together and are planning to raid his businesses for evidence. I'm sure we'll find something on him."

"Thank you for informing me of this," Chris said.

"It's generally not proper protocol to let someone who isn't with the police know about this, but considering how involved you and your catpanions are in this whole situation, it was the least I could do.

Officer Hudson agrees. Anyway, take care of yourself and be sure to keep an eye on the news. I'm sure you'll learn something good happened in the next few days."

As the woman hung up, Chris placed his phone in the gym bag, grabbed his towel, and headed for the shower while humming a merry tune. He couldn't wait to get home and tell Silva, Kuro, and Elsa the good news.

chapter 4

CHRIS WOKE UP EARLY the next morning to find both Silva and Kuro snuggling with him—or was he snuggling with Kuro while Silva snuggled with him? He couldn't rightly tell. Silva was pressed firmly into his torso, her naked body rubbing sensuously against him. On the other hand, he was basically resting against Kuro, using her massive tits as pillows. It was an odd situation that he'd been finding himself in more and more. Odd, but pleasant.

After spending a few minutes relaxing in bed, Chris knew it was time to get up. He removed himself from between Kuro and Silva and climbed off the bed. When he looked back, a smile appeared on his face. Silva had maneuvered herself after his warmth disappeared and was now snuggling with Kuro. Her much smaller body created a unique contrast between the two, which was only enhanced when combined with the difference in their skin color. He glanced at their breasts and entwined legs, then looked away.

He so did not need a boner right now.

Leaving the room, Chris washed his face in the washroom and walked into the living room, where he found Elsa sleeping on the couch. A pillow was tucked underneath her head as she lay on her side. The blanket she had wrapped around her body was a fleece blanket with the smiling face of a foxy woman saying "Hawa!" imprinted on it. She looked discontent, brow furrowed, lips set in a small frown.

Chris bit his lip as he knelt next to her and reached out. He brushed away some of the blonde bangs from her face, though he retracted his hand quickly when she turned over. As she did, the blanket covering her body parted, revealing that she was not wearing a shirt. Her breasts heaved as she shifted some more.

He found his eyes drawn to her breasts, which looked like they'd grown a lot since he last saw them. When had he last seen them anyway? Back when they were much younger, Chris and Elsa had taken baths together, but they stopped around elementary school after some kids found out and made fun of them for it. He didn't think he'd really spent any time looking at her body after that. Come to think of it, he had sort of distanced himself in terms of how intimate he acted with her around that time.

Regret tried to well up in his mind. If he'd only not let those kids get to him back then, perhaps he would have noticed her feelings.

Chris shook his head and leaned down, no longer hesitating as he placed a kiss on Elsa's lips. Her soft lips parted. Warm and pliant, lush and yielding, Elsa had the kind of kissable lips that most men drooled over. They were pouty and caused intense desires to well up in those who saw them.

At the very least, Chris could say he now felt those desires welling up when he gazed at her lips.

When Elsa didn't stir, Chris leaned down and kissed her again. A soft moan escaped Elsa's mouth, muffled though it was, and her eyes finally fluttered open as he pulled back a second time. Gazing into her sleep-addled eyes, Chris cupped her cheek and began rubbing her soft skin with his thumb.

"Morning, sleepyhead," he said.

"C-Chris?" Elsa yawned as she sat up, heedless of how her breasts were out for him to see. "W-what time is it?"

"It's… um…" Chris found himself gazing at her light pink areolae and slightly darker nipples. He didn't feel ashamed that he wanted to take those nipples between his teeth, swirl his tongue around them, and play with them—not anymore—but he didn't need the distraction right now. "It's still pretty early, about 6:30, but I'm about to get started on breakfast."

"And you're telling me this because…?" Elsa inquired with a sleepy glare.

"Because you were going to wake up soon anyway." Chris grinned as he cupped her cheek again. Finally, Elsa's eyes widened as he leaned forward. "And I figured I'd give you time to shower before the other two wake up."

He kissed her again, and Elsa's entire body went ramrod straight for all of two seconds before melting. She leaned forward and tilted her head. Chris had only been intending to give her a peck on the lips, but Elsa took his lower lip between her teeth and nibbled on it, then slipped her tongue inside of his mouth and rubbed their now entwined appendages together.

Chris had no idea how long the kiss lasted. Seconds. Minutes. Hours. All he knew was that the feeling of her tongue against his, of their lips firmly clamped together, sent an electric jolt straight through his brain.

He pulled back with a gasp, his breathing heavy, face flushed, as Elsa licked her lips. There was a smile so satisfied on her face that Chris thought she might have Cheshire cat blood in her.

"You have no idea how long I've been waiting for that," she told him.

"I think I do now," Chris admitted. He leaned over one more time, but this time he kissed her forehead. "Go hop in the shower. If you can finish early, I'll style your hair."

"Really?!" Elsa practically shouted, though she gave Chris no time to reply as she hopped off the couch and dashed for the bathroom.

Chris shook his head and chuckled as he stood up and made his way into the kitchen. The sound of the shower running came to him as he opened the fridge and looked at what they had. Eggs, milk, Greek yogurt, a bowl of fruit… after looking at everything in their fridge, Chris grabbed the Greek yogurt and fruit bowl, then took down some oats from a cupboard above the counter.

Whipping up a Greek yogurt parfait was fairly easy. He used regular water glasses and filled them with a layer of Greek yogurt, a layer of blueberries, followed by a layer of cooked oatmeal, and then another layer of Greek yogurt. He topped it with strawberry slices and chopped almonds. It was an extremely healthy breakfast.

The calcium and protein were more beneficial for a catgirl's bones than for a human's, and because

Greek yogurt went through a straining process to remove the whey, which was the liquid that contained lactose, it wouldn't cause a catgirl to get stomach cramps if they ate too much.

By the time Chris finished making breakfast and setting the table, Elsa came back out from the bathroom dressed in a bathrobe he'd bought for her. It was a simple pink bathrobe that went well with her fair complexion and blonde hair. At the moment her hair was damp, and a few trails of water glistened as they traveled down her neck and hair. One particularly adventurous droplet disappeared between her cleavage.

Just as he promised, Chris began combing Elsa's hair while she ate breakfast. Her cat tail waved back and forth with ecstasy as she munched on the Greek yogurt parfait. Chris knew that if he looked over her shoulder, he'd see her wearing a blissful expression. She was a big fan of tart foods.

He used a battery-powered curling iron to style her hair in ringlets. While he was working on her hair, a still half-asleep Silva wandered into the living room alongside Kuro, who released a loud yawn as she scratched her stomach.

"G-goooood morning," Silva mumbled as she wandered over to the table and sat down with a heavy plop. Kuro didn't even say that much. She just grumbled as she sat beside Silva.

"Morning," Chris and Elsa said at the same time.

While the two catgirls ate breakfast, Chris finished styling Elsa's hair, then sat down and ate his own Greek yogurt parfait. He glanced at the clock when he was done. 7:30 am. It was time for him to head out for school.

After giving all three catgirls a goodbye kiss, Chris grabbed his backpack and left the apartment.

***

The school day went by relatively quickly. It was Wednesday, which meant Chris had Catgirl Biology, followed by Quantitative Analysis, then Psychology.

Catgirl Biology passed simply enough as Professor Shinomiya lectured them on how a catgirl's body dealt with sickness and disease. The lesson was informative. Chris sat next to Anastasia and dutifully took notes. Quantitative Analysis and Psychology were nowhere near as interesting, at least to him, and it took everything Chris had not to fall asleep during these lessons. It didn't help that his teacher for Quantitative Analysis was pretty boring.

It was late afternoon by the time he finished

classes. Chris traveled to his kickboxing center. He planned to get his training in and end by sparring with Tanner, but he was surprised when, upon arriving, he found Kuro there and waiting for him.

"I'm surprised you came," Chris said. "You haven't come here since you and Silva were attacked."

Kuro looked magnificent in her black sports bra and skin-tight exercise shorts. Her muscular physique was on full display. The powerful abdominal muscles of her six-pack seemed to ripple as she twisted her torso while stretching, and her defined triceps flexed when every motion. Strong thighs glistened lightly with sweat, showing that she'd been working out for quite some time before Chris showed up. Her wild mane of hair was still let down, giving her a ferocious look.

She grinned at him, sharp canines glinting in the light.

"I normally wouldn't, but there's been a change in our situation. Go get dressed and I'll tell you about it."

Chris already knew it had something to do with Calvin Lafaard, which was the only thing it could have been in his mind, but he didn't say anything as he went into the locker room, dressed in his own workout clothes, and came back out.

What followed was Chris going through a basic set of stretches and exercises designed to limber up and work out his muscles. Once he'd built up a proper sweat, he and Kuro got in the sparring rink while Tanner watched on.

Chris adopted an orthodox fighting stance, while Kuro shifted into her odd military-like stance that looked like she was going to paw his face off. He still didn't understand how that worked. However, he already knew not to underestimate her.

As he took two steps into her guard, Chris ducked to avoid her jab, then attempted to pound her torso with two quick jabs of his own. Both were avoided when she stepped outside of his range. His attacks hit nothing but air.

"You remember what you told us last night?" said Kuro as she came in again, initiating the attack this time. Two swift punches screamed toward him, but Chris dodged one and blocked the other. The punches were followed by a powerful hook that Chris nearly missed. He bent his torso backward at the very last second, grimacing as he felt an epidermal layer of skin peel off his nose.

That had been too close.

"I remember," he said as he backed away and circled around Kuro, who turned to keep him in her sight. "What about it?"

"It turns out the police found a lot of evidence against Lafaard when they searched his house and place of business," Kuro informed him. "It was on the news this afternoon. Lafaard has been arrested for fraud, embezzlement, blackmail, extortion, and the use of gangs to incite violence. He might also have assault and murder charges filed against him, but that was only speculation. Either way, with Lafaard's arrest, there's no need for me to watch after Silva so closely."

Chris nodded as he raised his arm. A dull thud echoed in his ears as Kuro's powerful right hook slammed into his forearm, but he didn't let that stop him as he moved in and tried to launch a powerful uppercut at her chin. Kuro, however, must have been expecting it. She moved back, avoiding his attack. It helped that she was much taller. An uppercut was already hard to get on her because she was so much bigger than him. After avoiding his punch, she kicked him in the leg. Chris flinched as he went down. But he turned his fall into a roll and skipped back to his feet.

"And so you decided to come here and spar with me," Chris continued their conversation.

"That's right." Kuro was grinning, her cheeks flushed as an excited gleam appeared within her glowing green eyes. "It's been a while since we've had a chance to spar like this, and I haven't been able to really cut lose for a long time either."

It was true that she hadn't sparred with Chris since the incident. He could understand her desire to stretch her limbs.

Chris said nothing more as he darted forward and attempted to catch Kuro with a combination attack, but he was surprised when, after dodging his first punch, Kuro leaned low to the ground and launched herself at him like a jungle predator. She slammed into his stomach. A loud gasp escaped his mouth as the air was knocked from his lungs. He landed on his back, head striking the sparring ring. Stars exploded in his vision before he finally came to.

Only to find Kuro straddling his waist, pinning his arms to his side with her powerful thighs. She placed her hands on either side of his head and leaned down. The grin on her face sent a shiver up his spine, but it was not a shiver of fear.

"This is an awfully familiar position," Kuro said with a low chuckle. "Wasn't this how you lost to me the first time?"

"It was." Chris nodded. "As I recall, you got quite embarrassed when you realized how arousing this situation made me."

"That was then. This is now." Kuro didn't let the

memory of his erection poking her make her embarrassed. She leaned down further until their noses were touching. "Do you yield?"

Chris struggled to get out of her grip for a moment, but he quickly gave him. Not only had she completely pinned him in place, but Kuro was so much stronger than him, and her weight was pressing him down, that he couldn't move no matter how hard he struggled.

"I yield," he said at last.

"Good, then as the victor, I want to claim my reward." Kuro leaned down further. At first, Chris thought she was going to kiss him, but she moved to the side, and whispered in his ear. "I want you to take me on a date this weekend."

Chris's eyes popped wide open as Kuro stood up and walked off. After a few seconds, he sat up and gazed at Kuro as she left the ring and walked toward the door under the admiring gazes of basically everyone there. This place was filled with testosterone. It was only natural that men and women alike would enjoy the sight of Kuro and her incredible physique.

As Chris climbed to his feet and adjusted his gym shorts so his erection wouldn't be so visible, Tanner walked up to him. The buff man crossed his arms and raised an eyebrow at Chris. The look on his face, which was a mixture of smug and curious, caused Chris to look away.

"I've been wondering about this for a while now, but has Kuro become your catpanion?" he asked. Chris couldn't say anything, so he settled for a nod. Tanner scratched his head. "Huh. Well, sounds like you've got your work cut out for you. That woman looks like she's a hellcat."

Chris couldn't deny that.

***

The weekend eventually rolled around. During the weekday, Chris had been thinking hard about what kind of date he should take Kuro on. Going out to the movies was an old cliché that he'd rather not do, a picnic might be nice but it was still too cold, and while a brewery tour sounded fun, Chula Vista did not have that many great breweries. However, after thinking about Kuro and her active lifestyle, Chris finally came up with what he believed was a good date plan.

When Saturday afternoon came by, Chris stood by the door with a pouting Silva and a frowning Elsa. His shorts were the kind people wore when going to the gym. They were light and kept tight around his waist with simple drawstrings. Likewise, he was wearing a baselayer top that conformed to his body. He'd thrown a simple black jacket over his outfit.

"Are you still upset at me?" Chris asked the two.

"I'm not upset." Silva's cheeks swelled like a chipmunk's with too much food in them as she turned her head. "I'm just disappointed."

"You've never taken me on a date before," Elsa added, her frown growing.

Chris sighed. When he'd informed the two about his date plans with Kuro this weekend, the two catgirls had banded together and formed the pouting squad. While they didn't ignore him, they would occasionally make subtle jabs about how nice it was that he was taking Kuro on a date, and how sad they were that he'd never taken them on a date. It wasn't like he didn't understand where they were coming from, but he didn't think they had any right to blame him.

After all, the one who'd asked him to take her out was Kuro.

It wasn't long before Kuro herself emerged from the bedroom, wearing the same clothes she always did. Her carpenter pants had a very loose look. On the other hand, her sleeveless muscle shirt pretty much showed everything. Chris could even see the outline of her bra.

When Kuro stepped into the room, she paused and raised an eyebrow when she got a good look at him.

"Are you really taking me out on a date in that?" she asked.

"Are you really going out on a date with me in that?" Chris shot back.

Kuro looked down at herself, then laughed. "I guess you have a point. I don't really have the right to complain, do I?"

"You do not," Chris confirmed with a nod, then smiled. "Besides, the place I plan to take us for our date isn't somewhere you want to dress fancy anyway."

"Is that so? And you're not going to tell me where that is?" Kuro raised an eyebrow.

Chris shook his head. "Nope. It's a surprise."

As their back and forth banter continued, the pout on Silva's cheeks grew even more fiercely, until she looked like her cheeks had balloons stuffed into them. Elsa also looked put out, though not to the same degree. Chris was sure Silva was just upset because she'd been his catpanion longer and they hadn't gone on what either of them would call a real date.

To be fair, a lot had happened. Chris had never really thought about taking them on a date because, well, they had all been so busy. Were it not for Kuro basically demanding he take her out, he wouldn't have even contemplated the idea.

"All right. We're heading off," Chris said to the two other catgirls with a smile.

"Be good now," Kuro added.

With that, the two of them walked out of the apartment, closed the door, and made their way out of the complex and toward the nearest bus stop.

***

Silva and Elsa stood by the door as they listened to Chris's and Kuro's footsteps get further and further away. When the footsteps disappeared entirely, the two of them turned to each other.

"Nya ha ha! Are you thinking what I'm thinking?" asked Elsa.

Silva nodded. "If you're thinking of following them to see what sort of date they are going on, then yes, I am thinking the same thing you are."

"This isn't about being jealous that Kuro got to go on a date before either of us," Elsa added. "We're just concerned about their date."

"Right. We want to make sure their date goes well," Silva nodded, playing along with Elsa.

Their thoughts completely in sync, the two of them went into the bedroom and looked through the many cosplays Elsa had brought with her from home.

They needed to follow Chris and Kuro, to make sure the pair's date went well, but they didn't want the two discovering them. This was all for their sake.

They weren't jealous.

Not at all.

***

They stood before a long building shaped sort of like a stealth fighter plane. Palm trees and tarps stretched across metal poles dotted the landscape in front of the building. There were also several benches and areas to sit, but neither Chris nor Kuro paid any attention to those as the catgirl among the two gazed at the sign above a door that said "Skyzone Trampoline Park." With a raised eyebrow, she turned to look at him.

"This is where you plan to take me for our date?" she asked.

Chris grinned and shrugged. "The first part of our date, yes."

"A trampoline park? Really?"

"Don't knock it until you try it."

"I'm not exactly sure how going to a trampoline park constitutes a date." Kuro furrowed her brow. "Isn't this a little too... childish?"

"I like to bash the preconceived notions of what a date is until they look like something an elephant trampled over," Chris said.

"That was an awfully unusual analogy." When Chris just grinned at her, Kuro sighed. "All right. Show me what makes going to a place like this a good date."

"Don't worry. I will."

Taking Kuro by the hand, he led them inside of the large building. There were quite a few people present. Most of them were parents with their children, of course, but it wasn't like they were the only adults who hadn't come along with kids. As Kuro curiously looked at some of the people around them, Chris led her to the front desk, where a young man in his late teens or early twenties stood.

He greeted them with a smile, but it quickly left when he noticed how Kuro towered over him.

"Uh… hello," he said, his smile returning, though it looked uncertain now. "How can I, um, help you two today?"

"We'd like two tickets for ninety minutes," Chris said with a smile.

"Two tickets. Ninety minutes. Um, okay. Just… give me a second."

Kuro scowled as the young teenager fumbled to

get them their tickets, which only caused the poor boy to become more nervous. Chris chuckled as he held her hand and rubbed his thumb over her knuckles. The dark-skinned beauty's ears twitched several times as her tail curled. Her shoulders relaxed just a little.

Seconds later, the man set two pairs of thick socks on the counter.

"So, I need to go over the rules before you two can enjoy the Sky Zone." He glanced at Kuro, then quickly looked away. "First, you have to wear these skysocks at all times. No shoes. Make sure you empty your pockets of everything. We have lockers where you can stash your items like your wallet and keys away. Don't run onto the courts. Be sure to walk so you don't crash into anybody. While you can perform any number of tricks you want, you do so at your own risk. People have been known to get injured attempting to pull off a jump they couldn't do. Also, please make sure you are aware of the people around you at all times. Some people have been known to crash into each other while jumping. Finally, Sky Zone is not responsible for any injuries that occur because you didn't follow the rules."

"We understand," Chris said.

"In that case, your total comes to $40."

Chris paid for the tickets with his debit card,

grabbed the socks, and led Kuro away from the front desk. As he did, the young man behind the desk slumped his shoulders and wiped his brow. That caused Kuro's scowl to grow even more fierce.

"Coward," she grumbled.

"He was probably just surprised." Chris chuckled. "Not many people are used to seeing such an imposing woman, you know."

"Do you think I'm imposing?" asked Kuro.

"I think you're hot," Chris admitted, which actually caused Kuro to blush a little.

After finding an empty locker against the wall, Chris and Kuro emptied their pockets. Chris did raise an eyebrow when he noticed that Kuro had a knife hidden in her pocket, but she just smiled and shrugged as she set it inside of the locker. They removed their shoes after putting everything else inside. Once the locker was shut and locked, and they were now sporting a pair of thick and bright socks on their feet, the two made their way to the first attraction known as the Freestyle Jump.

There were already quite a few people bouncing around when they walked onto the massive trampoline. The shift from hard floor to bouncing trampoline nearly made Kuro stumble, but she was nothing if not graceful and caught herself before adjusting her weight to accommodate for the sudden change. Once they had found a place free of people, Chris turned to her and grinned.

"Ready?"

"No."

"Come on."

"No."

"Jump with me."

Despite her protests, Chris grabbed her by the hands and began bouncing. Kuro did not seem to see what was so fun—not at first. As time passed, Chris let go of her hands and began showing off, performing backflips and leaping from the angled trampoline wall to perform even more impressive aerial maneuvers. After finishing one particularly impressive axial body rotation, he glanced at Kuro.

"Are you just afraid I'll outperform you? Is that why you're not jumping with me?"

"That isn't it at all," Kuro grumbled as she crossed her arms. "I just don't think this is a good date. This wasn't what I had in mind when I asked you out."

"Uh-huh. I'm sure that's it." Chris shrugged and flipped again. "It's okay to admit you're not as good at me at something. There's no harm in admitting you lack my talent."

"Oh, that does it. You want to see how good I am?

Fine!"

Kuro narrowed her eyes as she leapt high into the air, came back down, bent her knees, and flew. As her body caught an extreme amount of air, she twisted herself into an even more impressive axial rotation than he had. Her body spun like a top as she rotated 360 degrees, then landed back on the trampoline with a bounce.

"There? You see that?"

"Now that's what I'm talking about!" Chris exclaimed with joy. "Come on! I'm challenging you to a bounce off!"

Despite her initial protests, as Chris continued pushing her into performing more incredibly complex acrobatics, a smile appeared on Kuro's face. It was a broad smile, the kind a person could only gain when they were thoroughly enjoying themselves. Sweat glistened off her body. Powerful legs and arms flexed as she pushed herself to outperform Chris. Her eyes were alight as she continued jumping, flipping, and soaring through the sky.

Because they had completely ignored everyone else, Chris and Kuro were unaware of the crowd that had gathered to watch them until loud clapping echoed across the trampoline. The two stopped what they were doing and turned. When they saw all the people clapping for them, they blushed in embarrassment, but still ended up showing off, performing more acrobatic maneuvers that most people would never be able to accomplish even with aid from a trampoline.

They didn't remain at the freestyle trampolines. Once Kuro began enjoying herself, Chris took her to the Skyladder, where they had to climb up a fidgeting ladder and reach the top. Chris fell several times, which caused Kuro to laugh at him before she showed off her catlike grace. She didn't even need to climb on her hands and feet. She walked along the ladder, all the way to the top, and planted her flag before turning around to grin victoriously at the scowling Chris.

"So you're a bit more graceful than me," he said with a huff. "I'll show you up at the Warped Wall."

"I don't know what that is, but bring it on," Kuro said.

Ninety minutes soon came and went. By the time they were done, Chris and Kuro were covered in a layer of sweat, but they wore broad smiles as they changed out of their skysocks. As Chris was getting their items out of the locker, Kuro sat on the bench next to it.

"Okay, that was fun," she admitted.

"I'm glad you had a good time." As Chris closed the locker, handed Kuro her shoes, and began slipping on his own shoes, a grin split his face. "Because this date still isn't over."

chapter 5

THEIR NEXT DESTINATION required them to travel via bus. As Chris and Kuro sat on the bus side by side, they found themselves being subjected to innumerable stares. A young girl was gawking at them, a pair of goths were staring at Kuro like she was a ferocious animal, and an elderly couple was smiling in their direction. The reactions their presence caused seemed to differ depending on things like age, orientation, and gender.

"Momma! Momma! Look at that huge cat lady!" a young kid spoke in an excited voice as he pointed at Kuro. The boy was sitting in the seat across from them.

"Don't be rude, Laiden!" The mother, a middle-aged woman with brown hair that had flecks of gray, scolded before casting a worried but polite smile at Kuro. "I'm sorry for my child's rude remark."

"It's fine." Kuro waved the woman's words off with a smile. "I am quite big, after all."

As the woman's smile grew less worried and

more relaxed, Chris glanced at all the different people sitting on this bus. There were quite a few. Like a melting pot, there were people of many different orientations, from Mexicans to Asian people to Europeans and everything in between. But as he continued staring, a pair of individuals caught his eyes and caused him to snort.

"I've noticed this for a while now, but I think we're being followed by a pair of nuns," he said with a chortle.

Kuro blinked at him, then looked around and found the nuns in question. They were sitting in the very back of the bus, dressed to the nines in long black and white habits. Their headdresses were quite large, big enough to cover their entire heads, though they didn't mask their faces from view, which of course meant Chris and Kuro could see who was hiding within those clothes. The heterochromatic blue and gold eyes were a dead giveaway for one of them.

"Those two," Kuro sighed and rubbed her face. "What the hell do they think they are doing?"

"Following us is my guess." Chris shrugged.

"What should we do?"

"Just leave them be." Chris gave his answer after a moment's thought. "I'm sure they will eventually get bored and head home." Kuro frowned a little, and

Chris could almost see the gears turning in her head. "With Calvin Lafaard under arrest, there isn't anyone who would go after them, and the catgirl protection laws are extremely strict. No one is going to break them to hit on a pair of catgirls dressed as nuns."

"I guess not."

While Kuro still looked reluctant, she conceded his point.

They got off at the next stop, which was a downtown strip mall with several expensive shops. Kuro glanced around curiously as Chris led her by the hand. The store they were traveling to was located inside of a large building composed of several other stores. It was called The French Gown. While it looked like any other store from the outside, the inside was much different.

"This is… are we going to buy me a dress?" asked Kuro.

Chris shook his head. "We're just renting. I sadly don't have the money for a dress like these at the moment."

The shop was tiny, with barely any room for them to walk. Most of the space was taken up by racks of various dresses. There were all manners of gowns, from dresses with rhinestones, to dresses that ended in fishtails, to expensive ballroom gowns that looked like they cost more than a blue-collar worker's yearly salary.

"I'm not sure any of these will fit me," Kuro said as she looked at the gowns. She bit her lip. "And I don't know if I'd look good in one."

"You'll look great in one. Trust me on this," Chris assured her.

As they spoke, a woman came out from the backroom and glanced at them. Curly blonde hair framed a young face that made it hard to determine her age. She presented an odd contrast to the gowns as she walked up to them, dressed as she was in jeans, a T-shirt, and sandals.

"Welcome to my shop. My name is Sally Lautus. Are you Chris Redford?" she asked.

"I am," Chris said with a smile.

"Oh, good. We've got the gown you ordered all ready for you." At these words, the woman glanced at Kuro with an appraising gaze, admiring her muscular physique. While she nodded, Kuro squirmed. "I can see why you needed to request a custom size. She is quite tall and imposing."

"Who's imposing?" Kuro muttered with some bite.

"Anyway, your dress is all prepared, so let's get you in the changing room."

"What the—hey! Don't push me! I can walk myself, dammit!"

Chris said nothing as Sally pushed Kuro toward the nearest changing room. He chuckled a little when Kuro almost hit her head because the door was too small. She had to duck just to fit inside.

He waited for Kuro to finish changing, glancing at his smartphone every so often. Out of the corner of his eye, he saw the two nuns, or rather, Elsa and Silva dressed in nun cosplay, hiding around a corner and gazing at him through the store window. Chris glanced at them. When he made eye contact, the pair squawked and disappeared behind the wall.

Another chuckle escaped his lips.

Finally, the door to the changing room opened and Kuro stepped out. She was wearing a scowl. Even so, Chris found his breath being stolen from him.

A simple but elegant black dress adorned Kuro's body. It had a modified halter neckline and cutaway shoulders that allowed her well-muscled arms and shoulders to be revealed in all their glory. The front had a gap around her chest, exposing just a hint of cleavage, while the back was sheer, allowing Chris to see bits of skin through the embroidery. A slit traveling down the left side of the dress not only made walking in it easier, but it also showed her powerful calves and thighs. The entire ensemble was finished with elegant strap-on sandals with slight heels.

"I look ridiculous," Kuro scowled.

"You look gorgeous," Chris countered.

His words stopped Kuro short. She glanced at him, blushed, looked away, and then crossed her arms. This had the effect of pushing her breasts together. Since they were so massive, it caused them to bulge.

Chris took a breath to calm himself down. He was going to get an erection if this kept up.

"I have to agree with Mr. Redford," Sally said with a smile. "You look quite lovely. You strike a very powerful yet elegant figure in a gown."

"W-whatever," Kuro muttered.

Because Chris had already paid for this rental dress, they didn't need to stay there, and they went to their next destination, which was right across the hall. It was a tuxedo rental shop. Once there, Chris spoke with the man in charge, and it wasn't long before he was dressed in a black and white tuxedo that matched her gown.

When she saw this, Kuro's eyes widened a little.

"I didn't realize men could look so good when they dressed up," she mumbled.

Chris grinned. "Does that mean you approve?"

Kuro nodded, unable to say anything else.

The tuxedo was rather simple when compared to Kuro's gown. It was a Calvin Klein slim fit tuxedo, which featured two buttons, a notch lapel, side vents, and flat-front slacks with a satin stripe down the leg. This rental had been sized to his measurements, so it did give him that powerful V-shape that showed off his lats.

"I'm glad this has your approval," Chris said with a smile before offering Kuro his arm. "Shall we?"

Kuro paused for a moment before sliding her arm through his. The expression on her face said she felt awkward, which might have been due to their incredible difference in height. Standing at somewhere around seven feet, Kuro towered over Chris by a good foot at least. On the other hand, Chris didn't mind this arrangement at all as he led her outside the shop, where an Uber—a Prius—was waiting for them.

He held the door open for Kuro, who climbed in, then glanced at the two catgirl nuns hiding behind a mailbox. Chris chuckled as he stepped into the Uber and sat next to Kuro. As the Uber drove off, he and Kuro glanced out the window. The two catgirls who'd been following them had stepped out from behind the mailbox and were standing in place, growing ever smaller as the distance between them increased.

****

Silva felt a number of complex emotions as she watched the car Kuro and Chris had stepped into disappear. She wanted their date to go smoothly, of course. She was very happy for Kuro, who seemed to be enjoying herself despite the numerous complaints they heard from her throughout the day. At the same time, she really wanted to go on a date too. She didn't like being left out. It was a complicated feeling.

"Nya ha…" Elsa sighed beside her. "What should we do now?"

"Let's… just go home," Silva said at last.

"Nya ha…"

****

It was later in the evening when they finally arrived at their destination, a large building of many stories that had several businesses located inside. The very top floor was their destination. It was a restaurant named Mister A's. As they entered the restaurant, a young woman looked at them with a professional smile and asked if they had a reservation.

"We do," Chris said. "It should be under Redford."

The hostess glanced at a tablet built on the front desk, scrolled through, and discovered his reservation. With another professional smile, the hostess stepped out from behind the desk and gestured for them to follow her.

"Please follow me. I'll show you to your table."

They walked behind the woman as she led them past several tables and the bar. Warm but low lighting provided a romantic ambiance as several patrons sat around small round or square tables, talking and smiling while sharing conversation, drinks, and food. They were led to a table near a window. The walls were made almost entirely of glass panels, which gave a grand view of San Diego at night. As they were seated, Kuro's eyes sparkled as she looked at the numerous lights from tall buildings that spread out to the event horizon.

"Beautiful," she whispered.

"Yes, it is," Chris said with a smile.

The hostess also smiled as she watched their reactions, seemingly pleased by how enamored they were with the view. Oddly enough, she didn't seem intimidated by Kuro's large size like some other people had been. He guessed she was just one of those unflappable individuals.

Maybe it was the dress…

"Your waiter will be with you shortly. In the meantime, please take your time looking at the menu. Our wine and cocktail selection is in the back."

"Thank you," Chris said.

As the woman left, a quiet silence filled their table as he and Kuro opened their menus and glanced at the options. Chris had turned to the cocktail selection. There were not too many options to choose from, but it seemed like they created specialized cocktails as opposed to simply giving many options.

"Would you prefer a bottle of wine or a cocktail?" asked Chris.

"Wine… I think," Kuro said after a moment. She blushed and looked away. "I've never really tried wine, or eaten at a fancy restaurant like this, but I have always wanted to do this at least once."

"Then I'm glad I could grant your desire," Chris said with a smile.

A man who looked a few years older than Chris came up, and while he did eye Kuro for a moment in shock, he was professional enough that he didn't let her imposing physique get to him. He introduced himself as Emile and said he would be their waiter for the evening, even as he poured water into their glass. When asked if they had decided on a drink, Kuro went with a cabernet sauvignon, while Chris ordered the

Cherry Blossom.

"Kind of a girly drink, isn't it?" asked Kuro with a teasing smile.

Chris shrugged. "I like sweeter drinks… and Toki whiskey is actually one of my favorites. Besides, if I was the kind of person who got worked up over something small like whether or not my drink was girly, I don't think I'd be the kind of person who could date such a strong woman."

"Th-that is true, I guess." Kuro looked away when his eyes bored into her. She seemed unusually vulnerable, but that was perhaps because she was so out of her element.

Kuro was a rough and tumble kind of woman, and some might have even called her wild. Her mane of hair, impressive physique, and obvious combat training gave her a sense of danger that would have caused most people to shy away from her.

They made small talk for a while. Chris asked about how Sister Ann and the catgirls at the orphanage were doing, and he was pleased to learn that the orphanage had been able to upgrade their furniture and equipment. Sister Ann had replaced the beds, tables, chairs, and just about everything else with brand new furniture, and she'd even managed to create a theater room for the kids to watch movies.

"After Calvin Lafaard was arrested, the money used for the GoFundMe project was given back to the orphanage," Kuro admitted. "We weren't sure what to do with that money at first, but Sister Ann decided to put it toward the orphanage and helping those less fortunate. Half the money went to a non-profit organization to help victims of abuse, while the rest was used to fix up the property."

"I'm glad everything worked out," Chris said. "I'm also happy that scumbag is in jail."

"Me too." Kuro smiled.

Their drinks came a few minutes later. While Kuro's drink was a rich and full-bodied red wine, Chris's was a light reddish pink liquid with a mixture of cherry jam, Spanish Vermouth, fresh orange, and Toki Japanese Whiskey. Despite poking fun of him, Kuro did admit that she enjoyed the beverage after demanding she try some.

After their drinks arrived, they ordered their food. They started off with plancha grilled octopus in romesco sauce. Kuro had never tried octopus before and was surprised by the taste. She ate more than half the dish herself, while Chris watched on with an amused smile that caused her to blush. Their meal after the entree was pan-seared ora king salmon for Kuro and snake river farm pork chops for Chris.

Both meals were delicious, and they ended up trying each other's food, though Kuro did blush heavily when Chris fed her. He thought it was cute how she tentatively leaned over the table and stuck his fork into her mouth. The way her eyes had lit up as she tried the pork belly had brightened the entire room.

They did not have dessert afterward, but they were both full. After leaving the waiter a sizable tip, they left the restaurant and began wandering through San Diego for a while, their arms locked together.

"When are we heading back home?" asked Kuro.

"Oh, we're not going back home tonight," Chris said with an amused smile.

While Kuro gave him a curious look, Chris just continued to grin mysteriously at her before he ordered another Uber, which took them through San Diego and toward a hotel: The Marriott Gaslamp Quarter. It was an elegant and upscale hotel in the middle of San Diego, with boutique-style service, sleek decor, and caught in the middle of the San Diego nightlife.

Just like with the restaurant, Chris already had reservations. Their room was a large guest room with a king-sized bed and a great view of the city. As she walked into the room, Kuro glanced at the sliding wooden door that separated the bedroom from a sitting room with a desk, several chairs, and a couch against the wall. There was a flat-screen TV across from the bed, situated in an alcove of the dresser, which made it perfect for watching movies while lounging on the bed.

"This place is nice," Kuro said.

Chris smiled. "Wait until you see the shower."

The marble bathroom had a shower/tub combination with water jets, large enough that Chris and Kuro could relax in it, and featured a detachable shower head. Given that he and Kuro had spent several hours at the Sky Zone sweating, they actually did need to take a shower.

Chris stripped out of his tuxedo and hung it up, making sure nothing was creased as he did so. He turned to Kuro after stripping and saw she was having trouble getting her dress undone. A smile appeared on his lips when he saw the scowl on her face. She looked incredibly put off, but he thought it made her cute.

"Here. Let me help you," he offered before reaching behind her and undoing the zipper hidden in the back. He helped slide the dress off her body, revealing the black lace undergarments she was wearing. Her bra and panties were a little more extravagant than he would have expected. In truth, he hadn't even realized she had such nice underwear.

"S-Sister Ann bought these for me when she found out I was going on a date with you," Kuro said with a scowl and a blush. "It's not like I wanted them."

"I didn't say anything." Chris raised his hands in a gesture of surrender.

"Your eyes say enough," Kuro stated flatly.

Chris could only smile sheepishly at her words before he removed his boxers. His half-mast cock sprang free, which Kuro eyed while licking her lips as she undid the catch on her bra. It was a front clasp bra, making it easier to undo. Chris could only admire her tits as they sprang free with a bounce. He didn't think he'd ever seen a woman with a more massive rack than Kuro. Finally, she removed her panties and revealed the trim patch of pubic hair just above her pussy. Chris sucked in a breath.

"Just as gorgeous as the first time I saw you," he mumbled. "I don't think seeing you naked will ever get old."

"I'm glad to hear that," Kuro said, having regained her bluster. She wore a predatory smile that revealed her sharp canines. "It would be bad for me if you got bored of me because I plan on never letting you go."

"I'm fine with that," Chris admitted as his cock slowly swelled at the sight before him.

Bereft of clothes, they entered the bathroom and turned on the hot water. It didn't take long for steam to rise. The heat caused a light sweat to break out on their bodies, but then they stepped into the shower and began washing each other.

Kuro allowed Chris to wash her unruly mane of hair, and once that was done, he took his time exploring her body. He reveled in washing her back, covered in powerful muscles that flexed as he moved his hands across them, then her tits, which felt heavy in his hands. The way his fingers sank into her breasts was incredible. They were at least four or five handfuls' worth.

Kuro's breathing became heavy and stilted as he played with her nipples, pinching and pulling and rolling them between his fingers. He didn't remain there for long though. He just wanted to get her worked up. After moving on, he enjoyed her stomach.

Chris hadn't really thought about it before meeting Kuro, but a woman with a six-pack was sexy as hell. The feel of her incredible abdominals caused a shudder to run through him. Some part of him lamented taking her out to a fancy restaurant instead of a nightclub, where he could have taken body shots off these abs.

"Y-you're incredibly thorough, aren't you?"

asked Kuro, her breathing hitching as Chris washed her legs and even her feet.

"I like to be as thorough as possible." Chris looked up and gave her an exaggerated wink. "We have to get as clean as possible so we can get dirty again."

Kuro snorted, but then she moaned when Chris teased her entrance, spreading her outer labia apart and gently stimulating her pussy and clit.

"Fuck! I can't take this damn foreplay anymore!"

Kuro groaned before she grabbed Chris by the hands and pinned him to the wall. With one of her hands, far larger than his own, holding his arms above his head, Kuro leaned down and planted a voracious kiss on his lips. Her tongue pushed past his lips and began exploring the inside of his mouth like an adventurer plundering for treasure. Chris tried to move his arms for a moment, but Kuro was far stronger than he was, so he gave up after a few seconds and just enjoyed the way she ravished his mouth.

As if just kissing him wasn't enough, Kuro pushed her body against his as she leaned down further. Chris felt his cock come into contact with her pussy as Kuro closed her thighs around him. It didn't go in, but she began grinding herself against his erection, which caused his dick to twitch.

"Kuro…"

"I said it before, didn't I?" Kuro leaned back and grinned at him. "That I'd take what I want from you, and that you should take what you want from me."

"I remember…"

That was about all Chris could say as she grabbed his cock in her hands and began stroking him. She applied more pressure than Silva did when giving him a handjob, but the difference in pressure only added to his pleasure. A white haze was cast over his mind as he tried to move his arms so he could reach her pussy. He wanted to please her as well, but Kuro wasn't letting him.

Kuro pulled back just as he was about to cum. Chris would have whined, but then Kuro turned around, spread her legs apart, and placed her hands on the shower wall as she leaned over. A single glance at her dripping wet cunt was enough to make Chris lose whatever might have been left of his resistance, if he had any to begin with.

"Are you just going to stand there?" asked Kuro, looking over her shoulder. "Come on and fuck me."

Chris didn't need any more invitation than that. He grabbed Kuro's hips, lined his cock up with her pussy, and thrust forward until he was buried to the hilt inside of her. Kuro released a pleased *"Yessss!"* that sounded almost like a hiss.

Because Kuro had told him to fuck her, Chris did, setting a relentless pace right from the start. The sound of his balls slapping against her echoed around the bathroom as he plowed into her from behind. Kuro's muscular ass shook as his hips struck them. He grabbed a handful of her plentiful rear end and roughly massaged her ass cheeks, which caused Kuro to arc her back and released a purring moan.

"Yes! Yes! Fuck me! Harder! Fuck! That feels— hyk! Feels so good!"

Chris thrust his hips even harder than before as he felt his balls and lower abdomen tighten. Because he wanted Kuro's orgasm to be even more powerful than his, he leaned his chest against her back, reached around, and placed a hand over cunt. He could feel his dick sliding in and out of her pussy, but he ignored that as he worked her clit from beneath its hood and pinched it.

"NNnggg! OH! FUCK!"

Kuro released a loud shout as her entire body shook and shuddered. Her cunt tightened around him as though trying to suck him dry, then he was releasing his seed inside of her. The moment only lasted for a few seconds. When it was done, Chris pulled his cock out. Even though it had grown slightly flaccid, the sight before him, of Kuro's pussy dripping with his cum, of her powerful back and shoulders heaving, made him fully erect once again.

"Let's take this to the bed," Chris said after using the detachable shower head to wash her pussy clean.

Kuro found this idea agreeable as she dragged him to the bedroom. She didn't even bother drying off as she pushed him onto the bed, straddled his waist, and began kissing him again. Their passionate and sloppy kissing caused saliva to well up inside of Chris's mouth, but this time he was prepared. He hooked his legs around Kuro's waist and used her unpreparedness to rotate them around. Now lying on top, Chris grinned into their kiss as he placed his hands on her tits and began kneading her breasts.

Perhaps it was because she was pleased by his actions, but Kuro let him stay on top as they made out. She moaned as he filled her mouth with his tongue. The slippery sensation of their tongues dancing together was electric. A heat filled their bodies and Kuro bucked her hips against him, as though responding to this burning need within her.

It wasn't long before they were fucking again.

Chris grabbed one of Kuro's legs and turned her onto her side. Kuro's expression, nose scrunched as she bit her lower lip and tried not to moan, set his soul ablaze. The way her tits bounced in this new position spurred him on further. He increased the speed of his thrusts, then slowed down, then sped up again.

"F-fuck dammit! W-what are you—hyk! What are you trying to do to me?!"

"Nothing! Just! Trying! Hn! To please you!"

Kuro's slippery insides rubbed against his cock in all the right ways. Her juices flowed around him and made it easier to really thrust himself inside of her. As Kuro's body arced and shook, her tail reached out and coiled around his left leg.

With the increased pace of his thrusts, Chris felt his body tightening again. It felt like every fiber of his body was going to explode. He tried to stave his orgasm off for as long as possible, but it really was no use. Kuro felt too amazing.

His cock exploded inside of her, releasing shot after shot of hot, sticky jizz. Kuro screamed when this happened, her thighs, calves, and stomach clenching as she came seconds after him. With her leg resting against his shoulder, Chris was able to see the way even her toes spasmed before completely going limp. Her leg rested on his shoulder as they both breathed deeply. After a moment, he set her leg on the bed and rolled Kuro over, admiring her.

Kuro looked stunning with her body flushed and

humming. Sweat and water from the shower caused her dark skin to glisten in the light. Her nipples were swollen and puffy from his actions. Half-lidded eyes gazed at him, set on a smiling face.

"That was nice," Kuro sighed. She seemed out of breath. "I guess it's good to occasionally let you take… take the lead."

"I'm glad you think so," Chris said as he crawled over to her and laid down.

"I think we should rest for a little bit," Kuro announced. "I'm kinda tired."

"Me too," Chris admitted.

"Just don't fall asleep," Kuro warned him. "If you do, then I'm just gonna fuck you while you sleep, and then you won't be able to enjoy it with me."

"Don't worry." Chris grinned as he leaned up and kissed her cheek. "I have no intention of falling asleep. Tonight is all about us."

His words caused Kuro to smile.

chapter 6

AFTER HE RETURNED HOME the next morning with Kuro, Chris found himself being tag-teamed by Elsa and Silva, who informed him in no uncertain terms that it wasn't fair for him to only take Kuro out on dates. Kuro had looked rather pleased by their reaction. However, Chris had only been able to give them a pained smile.

Thus the next Saturday and Sunday, Chris took them on their dates.

He ended up taking Elsa to a gaming event that was happening in Los Angeles, a tournament for a video game she had picked up recently and begun talking up. It was a battle royale game called *Apex Legends* that somehow became popular overnight. Chris hadn't had a chance to play it yet, but they had it for the Xbox One, so he and Elsa would likely be playing it soon.

Because of her shy personality, he ended up taking Silva to the zoo, where they both enjoyed a relatively quiet day walking around and looking at all the animals. Silva had been a particular fan of the elephants. They'd had lunch at the zoo, but then Chris pulled a similar stunt with her that he did with Kuro. He rented out some nice clothing, took her to a restaurant, then spent the entire night making love to her in a hotel.

The days after that passed by at a slow trot. Chris would wake up, go to college, go to his kickboxing center, and come home to a wonderful meal cooked by Silva. The silver-haired catgirl had become a master in the kitchen. She had surpassed his ability to cook certainly, but he also believed she had what it took to become a professional chef if that was what she wanted.

Like that, Chris's life seemed to have finally settled down.

***

The ringing of a bell signaled the end of class. As Chris, Anastasia, and the others stood up, Professor Shinomiya spoke to them.

"Remember, next week is the start of spring break, so you won't have any classes, but that doesn't give any of you an excuse to slack off. I plan on giving you all a quiz on everything you've learned in my class this semester. If I find that your heads have suddenly become empty over spring break, I'll be handing out extra homework."

Her words invoked a lot of groans from the class, but they didn't say anything against her. Everyone knew Professor Shinomiya really would do what she said. She'd done it before. After the winter break, she had given them all a refresher test to see what they remembered. When more than half the class had failed, she assigned them extra homework as punishment.

As they made their way out of the classroom, Chris and Anastasia walked side by side, talking about their upcoming plans.

"I'm actually thinking of heading back up to San Jose to visit my parents," Chris admitted. "I haven't seen them or my little brother in a while, and the only time I spoke to them over the phone was when I called to let them know Elsa was staying with me."

"You also need to introduce them to your new catpanions, don't you?" Anastasia asked with a shrug and a smile.

"Yeah… I'm not looking forward to that." Chris grimaced.

He loved his parents, and they were very kind and progressive people, but he felt they were maybe a little too progressive. If he brought Silva and Kuro home, they would overreact for sure. He could just imagine how his parents would talk about what a great, forward-thinking young man he was, and that they should celebrate his success with a party or some such nonsense. The last thing he wanted was a party celebrating his polygamous relationship with the catgirls in his life.

"What about you?" asked Chris. "Any plans?"

"I'm traveling to Mexico with some of my girlfriends." Anastasia's hair swished as she tilted her head from side to side, her eyes thoughtful but her smile playful. "They actually wanted me to invite you, but I didn't think you'd be interested." Her playful smile grew larger. "Plus, I think the others just wanted to spy on you having sex with your catgirls."

Chris almost nearly tripped over his own two feet, but he caught himself at the last minute. He glanced at his friend with wide eyes.

"Why would they want to spy on me having sex?"

"Oh, come on. Is it not obvious?" Anastasia rolled her eyes. "Do you not realize how insanely curious we women are? We want to know everything, and you're something of a hot topic right now, especially since it's become an open secret that you have multiple catpanions. My friends are curious to know what kind of sex life you have. They keep imagining all these kinky sex shenanigans. One of them even asked me if I knew where you lived."

"That…" Chris covered his face with a hand to hide his blush. "I don't even know what to say to that."

Anastasia smirked. "What? Not interested in sharing all your dirty secrets and bedroom activities with my friends?"

Chris glared at the woman, but that only caused her smile to widen.

They soon parted ways. Anastasia drove to school every morning, while Chris took a bus. He couldn't afford a car right now.

As he sat on the bus that would take him to the kickboxing center, he tried not to think about what Anastasia had said about her friends wanting to know what his sex life was like. People crowded in all around him. The scents from different perfumes, cologne, and one dude who smelled rank with BO pervaded his nose. While he was sitting and trying to ignore both the smell and his own thoughts, his phone suddenly rang. He pulled it out of his pocket and glanced at the caller ID.

It was Lacy Sutor of the Catgirl Protection Bureau's Office of Catpanion and Child Registration.

Chris blinked as he stared at the caller ID with a

dumb look on his face. How long had it been since he'd spoken with her? Probably almost a month now. Curious to know what this woman wanted, he accepted the call and held the phone to his ears.

"Ms. Sutor?" he asked.

"Hello, Mr. Redford," Lacy said from the other end. *"I'm sorry for calling so abruptly, but—what is all that noise coming from your phone?"*

"I'm on the bus," Chris said. "Did you need something?"

"Yes, two somethings actually," Lacy said, getting back on track. *"The first is that you need to schedule an appointment to take the Catpanion/Breeder Assessment Test soon. I was hoping we could find a time to pencil you in sometime during your spring break."*

"I don't mind. Does March 15th sound good?"

"That's perfect. Thank you." There was a pause from the other end. Chris imagined Lacy was inputting his scheduled assessment into her computer. *"Now, there are several certified Breeder centers where you can take this test. The one where you'll be taking the assessment test is near Chula Vista Harbor. I'll forward you their address via email."*

"Sounds good," Chris said. "You mentioned there was a second something I needed to do?"

*"Yes, and this one is going to be a little...
difficult."* Her words caused a small shiver to run
down Chris's spine, but he didn't say anything and let
the woman continue. *"I was going over your finances
recently. It seems you are currently living mostly off of
student loans. When you need to earn extra money, you
take creative commissions. Is that correct?"*

"Yes..." Chris said, no longer certain he
understood where this was going.

*"Are you aware that your student loans are not
meant to be used to house, feed, or otherwise take care
of catgirls? It is against the state policy that was set
down five years ago when someone tried to do
something similar to you and ended up using all the
money he had. Your student loans are meant for your
use and yours only. Now, while you can let catgirls live
with you, the extra expenses like dates, clothing, care
products, and so on must be paid with your own money.
Of course, food and medical products can be expensed
back to us, but you still have to pay for everything else
yourself."*

As the woman spoke, Chris vaguely remembered
hearing someone tell him something similar to this,
but it hadn't really stuck at the time. But now that she
had said it, he knew his current carefree days had come
to an end once again.

***

Chris returned home after a half-assed kickboxing training session. Tanner had not been pleased by his lack of attention, and Chris had paid for his inattentiveness with several powerful kicks to the ribs. Nothing was broken. That said, he would be sporting some lovely bruises tomorrow morning.

As he set foot into his apartment, Chris found about what he'd expected. Elsa was sitting on the couch and playing that new game she'd become so obsessed with. It looked like she was yelling death threats into her headset. Kuro sat next to her, watching the game as she sipped what appeared to be a beer. He wondered if maybe Kuro was interested in games like that. Maybe she was just bored.

"Welcome home, Chris."

Silva noticed his presence and walked out of the kitchen. She had a bowl of salad in her hands. It looked like a fruit salad as opposed to a regular one. There were all kinds of fruits like pineapple, strawberries, kiwi, bananas, oranges, blueberries, and grapes. It was a very colorful assortment. She walked up to Chris, leaned forward, and planted a kiss on his lips before moving over to the table.

"Thank you," Chris said, feeling a little better as the sensation of Silva's soft lips lingered on his.

Silva wandered over to the dining table and placed the fruit salad on the table. It looked like most of the table was already set up, as there were two placemats situated side by side on each side of the table, napkins, forks, and knives. The food hadn't been brought out, but as he breathed in the air, Chris could smell what was definitely baked chicken with a type of glaze.

"Nya ha ha ha! You stupid sack of shit! Do you think you can defeat me with those lame-ass skills?! Get down on your knees and repent!"

As he walked further into the apartment, Chris looked at Elsa as she trash-talked whoever she was playing against. There was a fanged grin on her face as she wore her magical girl outfit. She didn't seem to have realized he was there, but Kuro did.

"Hey, hon," Kuro said with a fanged grin. "Have fun at school?"

"I don't know if fun is the right word, but I learned a lot," Chris said with a shrug as Kuro took a sip of her beer. Seeing her so casually drinking beer reminded Chris of what Lacy had told him about his expenses, causing him to grimace.

"Is something wrong?" asked Silva, attentive as

always. She seemed to know when something was bothering him, perhaps because she had spent so much time observing him during their first couple of days cohabitating.

He smiled at her. "I'll tell you girls after dinner."

While it was clear that Silva was curious, she nodded in understand, then asked him if he could help bring in the chicken. He did so while Silva got Elsa and Kuro off from the couch. Elsa was a lot harder to pull away from her game than Kuro was. It took the silver-haired catgirl prying the headset off her head before Elsa stopped playing.

"Awww! Come on! I was kicking ass here!" Elsa complained.

"Dinner's ready," Silva said simply. "Also, Chris is home."

"Really?!" Elsa snapped her head around toward the dinner table as Chris placed the tray of chicken on a pair of heating pads. "Nya ha ha! Chris! Welcome home!"

"It's good to be—mph!"

Chris had very little time to prepare as Elsa scrambled off the couch, bounded over to him, and threw herself against him. Her lips quickly found his. The slightly citrusy taste of her mouth let him know she'd been drinking some kind of soda like 7UP...

though he wasn't sure where she'd gotten it. He wondered if she'd been sneaking off to the convenience store.

While he could have pushed her away, Chris did not do that. He wrapped his arms around her waist and kissed her back. The feeling of her lips on his, of her hands running through his hair, and of her breasts pushing against his chest, eased the tension he'd been feeling since Lacy's call… though it also caused a different kind of tension. Fortunately, Elsa was conscientious enough to not push herself onto him further right now. Silva would be most cross with her if she got Chris all hot and bothered right before dinner.

Dinner was an interesting time. Elsa did most of the speaking. She talked about how awesome the new game was, and how she was kicking everybody's asses. Chris was sure she was exaggerating. However, he never said anything against her since she spoke with such enthusiasm.

Silva talked to Chris about some of the new dishes she wanted to try making, which once again made him think about how she'd make a really good professional chef. She loved cooking. On the other hand, Kuro only made a few brief mentions about how the catgirls at the orphanage were doing. She wasn't really talkative when she was drinking.

After dinner, Chris cleaned and put away the dishes, and then asked everyone to gather in the living room. The three catgirls sat on the couch. He would have joined them, but he felt it was better if he was facing them for this conversation.

"It seems… we have a bit of a problem," he confessed.

"Nya ha ha! Have aliens invaded the Earth?"

"Are we running out of ingredients?"

"Has your libido gone down?"

Each of the three girls offered a completely different hypothesis on what the problem was, and all of them were so far off the mark that Chris wanted to facepalm. The only reason he didn't was that he'd been expecting this response. None of them had really thought about what being a catpanion meant, just like he hadn't considered what having catpanions meant.

"None of the above," Chris said. He ran a hand through his hair and sighed. "It seems we have a… small financial crisis on our hands."

"What does that mean?" asked Kuro.

"Are we out of money?" Silva furrowed her brow.

"Nya ha ha! Did you spend too much on porn?!"

"Where did that even come from?!" Chris snapped at Elsa. "You know I don't have any porn!"

"Relax, I'm just teasing," Elsa said with a grin.

Chris sighed at the catgirl, who was easily the most mischievous of the bunch, but he let her comment slide off him and explained the situation to them in detail. He informed them that while they could expense their food to the government, all the other things they were paying for had to be bought with their own money. Of course, this included clothing, hair products, toys, dates, and everything else.

This normally wouldn't be such a big deal, but there were actually a lot of things catgirls needed. What's more, because catgirls needed regular checkups, which also weren't paid for by the government, Chris needed to either put them on an insurance plan or pay for medical expenses out of pocket.

"Elsa is fortunately good. She's on my parents' plan," Chris said with a sigh. "But you two are not on any insurance plan. What's more, I can't put you on mine because I don't actually have one. Right now, I'm also on my parents' insurance."

"Can't we just go on your parents' insurance as well?" asked Kuro with a frown.

Chris shook his head. "Adding an extra catgirl to a person's insurance nearly doubles the monthly premium. There's no way my parents can afford to pay for two extra catgirls."

Those words caused a tense silence to fall over the group. Silva and Kuro glanced at each other with worry, but Elsa, who was already secure knowing she had insurance, merely looked smug.

"So, what should we do?" asked Silva.

"I'm thinking about getting a job," Chris admitted. "Commissions earn me a decent amount of money, but they aren't a stable source of income. In order to make enough for your bi-monthly checkups and such, I need a job that will net me at least $1,000 a month."

Chris had avoided getting a job because he didn't want to do something that would take away from his studying or exercise. Now that the situation had come to this, he didn't have much of a choice. If he wanted to provide for these catgirls, he needed money, which meant sucking up his distaste for getting a job.

Yet as he said this, the catgirls all looked at each other. Something passed between them that Chris couldn't understand. It was like they were talking to each other using nothing more than eye contact. He wondered if this was some kind of special catgirl ability, but he never got a chance to ask about it.

"I don't think it's right for you to be the one who has to work when you're already doing so much to provide for us," Silva said.

Kuro nodded. "Even though I don't live with you, you've given me a lot and helped me and my friends out whenever we've needed it. You're doing more than enough for us."

"Nya ha ha! While I am on your parents' insurance plan that doesn't mean I'm just going to sit by while you're facing this financial crisis!" Elsa placed her hands on her hips and thrust out her chest.

Chris blinked. "I'm not sure I understand. Are you three saying…?"

"We're saying that rather than having you get a job, the three of us are going to look for a job," Silva announced, shocking Chris.

"You don't have to—"

"You're right. We don't have to," Kuro interrupted, her smile gentle. "We aren't doing this because we need to. We want to help you. After everything you have done for us, this is the least we can do for you."

"For a while now, I haven't felt like we've had an even partnership," Silva added. "You provide me with a home, pay for all my food, give me a lot of love, and made me remember what it feels like to have a family. You've given me so much, but all I've done is warm your bed and cook meals. I want to do something more to provide for you—no, I want to provide for us."

"I'm already used to working for your mom." Elsa shrugged. "Finding more freelance work won't be a problem for me. And it'll give me something to do besides just sitting at home and playing video games, nya ha ha!"

Chris needed a moment to really think of a response. He was naturally happy they wanted to help, but a part of him, his stupid male pride, felt like he should be the one providing for them and not the other way around. However, he also realized stupid male pride never got people anywhere in life. His catpanions wanted to do something for him, wanted to help provide for this family. What kind of man would he be if he got in the way of that?

He was also happy to see how independent these three were, especially Silva. Unlike Elsa, who had never faced the kinds of hardship the other two had, and Kuro, who had military training and was incredibly disciplined, Silva was just a normal catgirl until her Grams died and she was taken by Markus. When she had first started living with him, Silva had needed to constantly remain by his side and couldn't go out without him around. Now she was talking about working.

"Do you girls have any idea of what kind of job you're going to get?" asked Chris as he slowly accepted the idea. This was something they had decided for themselves. He didn't want to let his own ego and misplaced desire to protect them get in the way of that.

"I want to get a job that involves cooking!" Silva said with enthusiasm.

"Nya ha ha! You know I'm going to find some work as a freelance programmer!" Elsa laughed.

Kuro shrugged. "I'm not sure. Maybe I could become a bouncer?"

"I don't think there are any bouncer jobs in Chula Vista," Chris responded to Kuro's comment with a wry smile. "Also, I think you should get a job at the same place Silva works. I'd feel better knowing someone was there to look out for her."

Silva's cheeks puffed out as she pouted at him, but Chris wasn't going to let this go. He was more than happy that she wanted to begin working. It was a huge step and one he believed would be good for her, but he still wasn't comfortable with the idea of her being alone. Kuro was strong. She could protect Silva even better than he could.

Kuro furrowed her brow, then sighed and crossed her arms. "I guess I could get a job waiting tables if Silva works at a restaurant." She shrugged. "Not sure they'd accept such a big woman, but we'll see."

And that was pretty much the end of their discussion. After that, Elsa, Kuro, and Silva began searching for jobs while Chris went to college.

Elsa was the first one to find a job, and just like she'd said, her job was freelance programming and web design. He hadn't realized it, but Elsa apparently had some connections thanks to the work she did for his mom. Not only did she have connections, but Elsa had her own LinkedIn account, which she now put to use. She used her connections to get six jobs lined up within two days.

Silva and Kuro had a much harder time.

The biggest problem with finding a job as a chef was that a lot of other people also wanted to be chefs— and most of them had an actual degree. In fact, it was apparently quite rare in this day and age for someone who hadn't gone to culinary school to become a chef. The difference between a chef with a culinary degree and one without was sometimes a deciding factor in whether or not someone became accepted.

Silva applied for several places but was turned down in favor of chefs with an associate's degree in cooking.

"This is a lot harder than I thought," Silva confessed on March 14th, one day before Chris needed to take his assessment test to make sure he was physically and mentally fit to have catpanions. "I haven't even gotten called in for an interview. Most places just send me an email saying they already found someone or claiming I lack experience or they can't hire me because I don't have a degree in cooking."

They were sitting on the couch in the living room. It was just them right now. Elsa was working away in the bedroom where it was quiet and Kuro was… well, he didn't know where she was. Probably at the orphanage to check on the other catgirls. That meant they were alone.

Silva was leaning into his side, her tail coiled around his left arm as she rested her head on his shoulders. Her ears were drooping as if emphasizing the sadness she felt. Chris thought he understood how she felt. He had not personally experienced this vicious cycle that was getting a job, but he knew a lot of friends who complained about how difficult it was finding work. Even some of his fresh out of college friends had mentioned how hard it was.

As he thought about her problem, Chris wondered if there was some way he could help her out. He knew she wanted to find this job on her own. Silva wanted to prove that she could also provide for them. He understood that desire. At the same time, getting a job when you had no experience, no degree, and no reputation was difficult. If only there was someone who could help… them…

"Ah," he muttered.

"What?" Silva raised her head. "What 'ah'? Did you think of something?"

"I have, actually." Chris grinned as he leaned back to look into Silva's blue and gold eyes. "I just realized that we actually know someone who is a strong advocate of catgirl rights and would probably be more than happy to help you find a job."

"We do?" Silva asked before her own eyes widened. "You mean…?"

"Yes. I think we should speak with Anastasia and see if her mom could help us get you and Kuro jobs," he said with a gleam in his eyes.

chapter 7

"YOU WANT SOMEONE to help your catpanions find a job?" asked Anastasia as she sat with Chris at the Starbucks that had become their regular gathering spot after Catgirl Biology class.

Despite the fact that Chris had turned her down, Anastasia continued to treat him like a good friend. Actually, she seemed to be even more friendly with him than before. She chatted with him more often, shared complaints and stories with him whenever they had some free time, and basically treated like him a… well, he didn't want to say she treated him like a girlfriend, but she definitely didn't treat him like a guy she wanted to date.

"I don't need help with Elsa," Chris said as he stirred his caramel macchiato with a stirring rod. "She already has several jobs line up, or so she says, but Kuro and Silva have never tried getting a job before."

Kuro had worked in the military for a time, but that was the extent of her experience. She'd never gotten a normal job working at a restaurant or anywhere else. Without that experience and a good resume, there was no way she would be able to get a job.

"Well… I suppose I could help you out," Anastasia said with a sigh. "I know a few agencies who work with my mother. Their goal is to help catgirls find jobs in their chosen professions. I'll call them and let them know they should get in touch with you. In the meantime, you should head to their website and fill out some forms for your catpanions."

She gave him the name of the website, www.CGWork.org, then spent the rest of her time complaining about how her friend was complaining about her newest boyfriend. Chris listened to her with the same attentiveness he'd show his catgirls when they spoke… even though he wasn't interested in her friend's boyfriend or what was wrong with him. They parted ways several minutes later.

After school, Chris made his way to his kickboxing training, where he spent a good hour working out and sparring with Tanner. Then he showered, dressed in his normal clothes, and took a bus back home. It was early evening when he arrived.

Silva greeted him with a kiss. Kuro did too, but her kiss felt more like she was trying to dominate his mind, body, and soul. Elsa was the only one who didn't kiss him, but that was because she was busy playing on her PSP. That said, she did greet him when he sat beside her.

That evening, Silva made another one of Chef Gordon's specialties: Stuffed roast chicken. It was a chicken roast stuffed with chorizo, onions, garlic cloves, semi-dried tomatoes, and who knew what else. Chris didn't know how it was made of, exactly, but it tasted delicious. The chicken was tender and juicy, not at all dry, and the chorizo, bean, and tomato stuffing helped the chicken cook evenly and perfumed the meat. She served it with steamed vegetables that had been lightly seasoned with salt and pepper.

Later that night, Chris had all the catgirls sit down around him on the couch as he used Elsa's laptop to go onto the website that Anastasia had told him about and created an application for Silva and Kuro. It only took an hour. Once that was done, everyone brushed their teeth and got ready for bed.

✳✳✳

The next day was Saturday, the beginning of spring break. The first thing Chris did after making everyone breakfast that morning was check Silva's and Kuro's applications to see if they had been processed. They had. It looked like the forms had been processed sometime last night. When he checked on the website, Chris noticed that there were already several job listings for the positions they wanted.

Both were going to work in the food industry, but Kuro was going into what would be deemed customer service (waitress/hostess), while Silva wanted to be a chef.

"It looks like there are several positions for Commis Chef available," Silva said as she and Elsa sat next to him on the couch. Kuro was sitting at the table and sipping a cup of black coffee. When he glanced at the woman, he noticed how the robe she was wearing had parted around her massive breasts, revealing her dark cleavage. She also sat with her legs spread, but that was just how Kuro sat.

"It looks like to apply for a position, all you need to do is click on the job you want to apply for and your resume immediately gets sent to that company," Elsa murmured. "Nya ha ha. That's pretty convenient."

"It is, but the problem is that Kuro and Silva don't have much of a resume since they lack experience," Chris said with a sigh. "Most places won't hire a person that lacks experience unless they are willing to work at the bottom of the barrel. For Silva, that would mean being the one who cleans the dishes instead of cooks."

"I-I don't want that," Silva said, her eyes wide.

"That's just how it generally works," Chris informed her. "Since you're a catgirl, you do have a few privileges that other people don't. I think there is a ratio where a company has to hire a certain number of catgirl employees, though it might depend on the type of business and the position you're applying for."

"Nya ha ha! Let's just have Kuro and Silva apply for all of them," Elsa said as she tapped on her laptop, which was a touchscreen, and hit the application button for every single position available. Chris twitched. Some of these jobs were located over an hour from their house.

He sighed. His blonde catpanion could really be a handful sometimes.

As this thought crossed his mind, Chris's cellphone started vibrating in his pocket. Standing up, he let Silva try to stop the laughing Elsa from sending her application to every job under the sun and walked into his bedroom. The last thing he heard of the two was about what he'd expect.

"S-stop hitting the application button!"

"Nya ha ha! What's the problem? If you want to get a job, you can't afford to be picky!"

Shutting the door to his bedroom, Chris looked at the caller ID. It was his mom.

"Hey, Mom," he said after accepting the call.

"Hey yourself," his mom said. *"Do you know how hard it is to get ahold of you? You never call home. I figured since you weren't keeping in touch with me, I should get in touch with you."*

"Sorry about that," Chris apologized. "Things have been kind of hectic here."

"I know. You might not be keeping in touch, but Elsa has been."

"Ah."

"Listen, I wanted to know if you were planning to come back home for Spring Break. You know we miss you."

"I know," Chris said softly. "I was actually planning on coming home, but a small problem has come up."

"Do you need help?"

"I think we can handle this. It's just a little financial issue. My catpanions are currently in the process of applying for jobs to help me out. That's why I can't come back home for spring break."

"You always were a very progressive thinker," his mom said. Chris rolled his eyes. *"And don't roll your eyes at me."*

"I didn't."

"So you say, but I don't believe you. A mother's intuition is not something you can underestimate. Anyway, it's fine if you can't come back right now. Do what you have to. However, I do expect you to come home during the summer holidays, and I expect you to introduce us to all of your catpanions."

"I will," Chris promised.

"Good. Talk to you later, sweetie."

"Bye, Mom."

Chris sighed as he hung up the phone and placed it back in his pocket. He didn't blame his mom for calling him. It was his fault for not calling her in several months. Ever since Silva arrived in his life, he'd been dealing with one incident after another.

"Chris?"

Turning around as the door creaked open, Chris looked at Kuro as she entered the bedroom. Her bare feet padded along the carpet. The robe was still parted to show an obscene amount of her cleavage, but she didn't seem to care, so who was he to complain?

"What's up?" Chris asked.

"Nothing." Kuro shook her head. "I was just wondering who was calling you."

"That was my mom."

"Oh." Kuro's eyes widened before she settled

down again. "I guess you would have a mom."

Chris frowned. "What's that supposed to mean?"

"Nothing." Kuro waved off his look with a grin. "Anyway, you might want to come back into the living room. Silva and Elsa are climbing all over the furniture."

At that very moment, as if to emphasize her words, a loud crash echoed from the living room. Chris looked at the wall as if he could see through it. Then he looked at Kuro, whose bright grin showed off her sharp canines.

He sighed.

***

Chris woke up with a pleasure-filled gasp as something warm, wet, and slightly rough licked the underside of his shaft, going all the way from his balls to his head. An electric feeling coursed through him. His eyes snapped open. He felt disoriented at first as he found himself staring at a ceiling, but then another jolt raced through his body like a bolt of lightning, causing him to look down.

Brilliant blue eyes surrounded by gorgeous blonde hair stared at him mischievously. The beautiful Birman catgirl truly looked like the cat that ate the canary as she straddled his legs, her mouth full of his cock. She hummed. The vibration sensation of her actions caused Chris to grit his teeth as his balls twitched. That twitching grew when a soft hand reached out to fondle them.

"E-Elsa…" he gasped softly, trying his best not to make too much noise.

Sleeping beside them was Silva and Kuro. The two catgirls lay on his left and right respectively. As always, Silva was completely naked, her small body pressed against his, holding his arm close. Her eyes were closed and her breathing deep and even. It was a wonder she hadn't woken up. Kuro, on the other hand, was snoring loudly and lazily. He actually thought he saw a snot bubble erupting from her nose.

"Mmm hm hm hm… mmm…"

As she finished laughing around his dick, which truly sounded odd, a slurping sound that seemed unusually loud echoed around the room as Elsa removed his cock from her mouth. It was painfully erect. When he looked down, he could see how the veins of his cock, covered in Elsa's saliva, were throbbing.

"W-what are you…?"

Chris's mind was out of sorts. He blamed it on waking up to such an incredible feeling. His mind couldn't keep up with the pleasure he was experiencing.

That confusion only increased when Elsa hefted her large breasts and pressed his dick between them. As he was engulfed in the incredible warmth of her chest, Elsa began moving, furiously rubbing him with her gigantic tits. He breathed in deeply through his nose and bucked his hips.

"Do you like that, Chris? Do you like it when my tits are wrapped around your dick?" asked Elsa with a smile that went beyond words like seductive or sexual. He'd never expected to see such a look on her face. Even so, he couldn't deny that her expression just then was almost enough to make him cum on the spot.

"I… I do," he gasped. His dick was twitching again. If she kept this up, he'd definitely cum!

"I'm glad to hear that," Elsa said as she continued giving him the greatest titjob he'd ever had in his life. The sensation was slightly slimy because he was coated in her saliva, but that only made it easier for her to slide his shaft along her breasts. "I want you to cum all over me. Cum. Shoot your white-hot jizz all over my body and face, Chris. Do it now."

When did she learn to talk like this?! That was something Chris wanted to know really bad, but his mind could barely even formulate the question. Those words were his breaking point. Releasing a constrained grunt, he exploded all over Elsa's chest and face, splattering her with his seed.

As Chris gasped and tried to recover his breath, Elsa leaned back and smiled as she massaged his cum into her chest. He blinked several times. In that time, Elsa had scooped some of his seed onto her finger and licked it clean. As he watched her erotically swirl her tongue around his mouth, Chris's dick sprang back up like a soldier standing at attention.

Elsa's eyes gleamed. "Nya ha ha. I knew it was only a matter of time before you realized my charms, Chris."

Chris, despite feeling like he'd just run a marathon, managed to smile. "I'm only sad I didn't recognize them sooner."

"As well you should." Elsa pawed at his cock like a cat testing out a new scratching post. He twitched, but she just grinned at him. "What should we do about this?"

"N-not here," Chris muttered. "I don't want to wake the others."

"Too late," a voice said to his left. "We're already awake."

A pair of beautiful eyes, one gold and one blue, appeared in his field of view, surrounded by gorgeous silver hair. Silva wore a catlike smile as she stared at him.

"When did you wake up?" asked Chris.

"A little while ago," Silva admitted as Kuro sat up on his other side and blinked at the trio. "It's kind of hard to stay asleep when such a strong scent fills my nose."

Was she saying he smelled?

"Um… Sorry?"

"Don't be." Silva leaned in close. "I rather like it… your smell."

Chris didn't have time to ask her what she meant before Silva's tongue was invading his mouth. He tried his best to keep up with her, but then a warm, wet, and incredibly soft pussy engulfed his cock. Elsa was riding him. He bucked his hips into her, which caused Elsa to release a loud cat-like purr as she leaned back, tits bouncing freely as she rode him to orgasm. He felt when her walls clamped down around him. Her juices leaked all over his shaft, thighs, and the bed as she came. However, he was still hard.

"Oh, my. Nya ha ha. It looks like Chris isn't going to settle down with just that," Elsa said with a fiendish smile.

"Perhaps I can help calm this raging beast," Kuro said, playing along.

"So we're slaying the dragon?" asked Elsa.

"Something like that."

Chris couldn't even ask what they meant because Silva continued to kiss him, and he was getting lost in the taste of her soft and succulent lips. He reached out and threaded his hand through her hair, grasped the back of her head, and tugged her closer to seek out more of that beautiful mouth. Their tongues swirled together in a dance as Silva placed her hands on his chest and felt him up. He grunted when she began playing with his nipples.

He didn't think he could feel any more pleasure, then something incredible engulfed his dick again. It felt like when Elsa had given him a titjob but times two. When he opened his eyes, Chris could just vaguely see both Kuro and Elsa on either side of him, pressing their breasts together, with his cock in between them.

It was too much.

Groaning into Silva's mouth, he released another load of his seed all over Kuro and Elsa. Several spurts coated their tits and a bit of their faces. When Silva leaned back to look at them, he gasped and tried to regain his breathing, but all three girls seemed to think giving him a show was a great idea.

They began licking each other clean.

Chris had seen a lot of erotic stuff in his life—normally from the porn he used to watch as a teenager—but the sight of Silva licking the cum off Elsa's nipples, of Elsa and Kuro sharing his seed between them in an open-mouthed kiss, their tongues swirling together, was far too erotic. It was easily the hottest thing he'd ever seen.

His dick came to life again.

"Oh, it looks like he's ready for round three," Elsa said with a smile.

"I'm next," Silva demanded.

"Tch. I guess you were his first catpanion. You're lucky I love you so much," Kuro said.

As Silva nearly giddily mounted him and began riding his dick like a cowgirl, Chris wondered if they realized he needed to be healthy and not exhausted for his assessment and evaluations today.

Probably… not.

***

"Sorry, Chris."

Three apologies rang out from his catgirls, but Chris was not in the mood. He sat with his head on the dinner table. His body felt like it had been run through a blender. He was so sore it wasn't even funny, and he was exhausted… it was almost like he hadn't gotten eight hours of sleep the previous night.

"Ngg…" He groaned, turned his head to the side, and looked at the closest person to him—Kuro—with a mild glare. "I love you girls, really, but you know I have my assessment today. I really don't need you draining me dry." He paused long enough to shift in his seat. "And my dick now feels raw. I think they have to take urine and sperm samples for this. What will you three do if I fail my test because I'm puffing out powdered milk?"

Three heads were hung in depression.

"We're sorry."

He sighed. "It's fine, I guess."

Chris wondered if he was being too light on them, but it wasn't like he could really complain about his situation. Two hours' worth of wake-up sex was fun. He couldn't lie and say he hadn't enjoyed it immensely. That said, he was still worried about his performance during the assessment…

"Anyway…" He raised his head and looked at the girls. "You two have a job interview today, right?"

"That's right." Silva perked up at his words. "We have an interview with Italianissimo Trattoria. It's actually within walking distance from here, so we won't need to take a bus or anything."

"We were pretty lucky I saw a flyer that said they were hiring," Kuro added. "That website your friend set us up with hasn't been very helpful in finding either of us a job."

"I'm glad you've got that interview lined up." Chris smiled before turning to Elsa. "And what are you gonna be doing today?"

"Nya ha ha. I'm working as an independent contractor for a third-party software developer," Elsa explained as she puffed out her chest. "My current job is testing a new program designed to transfer data between other software. I need to make sure there aren't any bugs or programming errors so the data transfers over from one program to the next smoothly. I also need to update the software as needed to enhance its performance."

It always impressed Chris when Elsa explained some of the things she did. He didn't understand half of it. It was like she was speaking an alien language, but that was what made her so impressive. She understood something only a few people did, and she hadn't gone to school or college for it. This was stuff she had discovered on her own through trial and error.

"Well, I'm glad everyone has a plan today," Chris said with a sigh.

"Nya ha ha ha! Don't worry about me. I'll be

staying home all day."

"We should be fine too," Kuro added.

"Good luck on your assessment," Silva said in a soft voice.

"Thanks," Chris said with a wan smile. Given that he felt like he'd been drained of all his life essence, he had a feeling he'd need luck to pass these assessments.

****

Chris's assessment was set for 10:00 am, so he left not long after eating breakfast. His destination was known as the Chula Vista Catgirl Breeder Center. He needed to hop on the monorail to get there, and it was about one hour from his apartment complex. Most of that time was spent watching *Hunter x Hunter* from his phone as several people, young and old, sat beside him.

The Chula Vista Catgirl Breeder Center was a fairly sprawling complex composed of numerous buildings bundled together behind a wall. There was only one gate used to get inside. After giving his name to the security guard standing at attention inside a security booth, they checked to make sure he had an appointment, then let him in.

Because Breeders were carefully regulated, anyone who became a Breeder was required to live inside of a Breeder center like this one, which Chris thought explained why this complex looked more like a resort than a simple business center. Several of the buildings had a very Mediterranean feel to them. Meanwhile, the grassy fields had trees sparsely populating them and paved walkways meandering throughout. Chris stopped for a moment when he spotted a beautiful flower garden with hundreds of differently colored blossoms.

He was not the only one present. There were several human men along with a number of catgirls. Many of them walked arm in arm and spoke in hushed tones and soft giggles.

These men were probably Breeders, a group of human males who had passed rigorous tests in order to become someone capable of satiating a catgirl when she went into heat. Chris glanced at one particular man who wandered by. He shifted his gaze from the blonde pretty boy to the girl beside him. This catgirl was a Maine Coon. She was larger than most girls, had a massive bust, and golden eyes. Her tail was curled around the Breeder's leg and she was affectionately rubbing herself against him.

She was obviously in heat.

Chris shook his head and continued.

His destination was the largest building in the very center, which looked like a giant dome, or maybe an amphitheater with a domed ceiling. He walked through a pair of sliding doors and entered a lobby. There were several people inside. Most of them were catgirls who were in the process of filing applications to have a Breeder satisfy the itch they needed someone to scratch. Ignoring them, Chris walked up to the front desk.

"Excuse me," he said to the young man sitting behind the desk. "My name is Chris Redford. I'm here for an appointment."

The man looked up at Chris, gave him a once over, then typed his name into a computer. Chris waited patiently as the man scrolled through several pages. He couldn't see what was going on, but he assumed this receptionist was looking for his name.

"Chris… Chris… Chris—ah ha. We have you on file," the man said, narrowing his eyes slightly. "It says you are here to take a catpanion assessment with Dr. Slate." He looked up and smiled. "I'll let him know you're here. In the meantime, feel free to sit down and wait for him to arrive. It shouldn't be too long."

"Thank you."

Chris turned around and walked toward a padded

chair next to the table. There were several magazines scattered across the table, but he didn't pay attention to them. Instead, he placed a set of earphones in his ear, accessed his Crunchyroll app on his phone, and began watching anime again.

Like that, several minutes passed. Chris managed to get through an entire episode of Hunter x Hunter before a man wearing a labcoat, black slacks, and a brown shirt walked in. He appeared middle-aged. His brown hair had flecks of gray, his skin was slightly wrinkled, and he had crows' feet around his steel eyes.

"Chris Redford?" he called for Chris as he looked at a tablet in his hand.

Chris stood up and walked over to him. "That's me."

"I'm Dr. Slate," the man introduced himself as he stuck out his hand. Chris took it. "I'll be the one administering your catpanion assessment test."

"It's a pleasure to meet you," Chris said.

They walked through a door in the back, which led into a hallway that looked like something he'd find in a hospital. Several men were wandering through this hall. Most of them wore labcoats and looked like scientists, but a few of them were virile young men who were undoubtedly there with the hopes of becoming a Breeder.

As they walked, Dr. Slate informed him about his assessment.

"Catpanion assessment tests are basically the same test men who want to be Breeders undergo. You'll be tested physically, mentally, and emotionally to make sure you are stable, well-intentioned, and capable of satisfying your catpanions. We will also need DNA samples, including hair, skin cells, urine, and sperm samples."

"I knew it," Chris groaned.

"Pardon?" Dr. Slate asked.

"Nothing," Chris said, shaking his head.

Chris was soon led into a small room that had a number of monitors and computers, which he recognized as equipment meant to monitor a person's heart rate and other vitals. He was asked to strip off his shirt. Then Dr. Slate attached several nodes to his chest, back, arms, legs, and forehead. After that, he told Chris to run on the treadmill.

This wasn't the only physical assessment Dr. Slate had Chris do. While hooked up to numerous devices, Chris underwent a variety of different exercises meant to test everything from his physical strength to his lung capacity. The doctor even had him submerged in a large vat of water, told to hold his breath for as long as he could. A number of these tests made very little sense to Chris.

Finally, the test he'd been dreading the most arrived.

"We need a sperm sample now," Dr. Slate said, holding out a cup.

Chris stared at the cup like it was his most hated enemy, but when Dr. Slate gave him a look, he had no choice but to sigh and take it. The cup felt heavy, even though he knew it probably didn't weigh more than a few ounces. This was not a physical weight. It was the weight of his worry.

"Do you have a bathroom or something I can do this in?" asked Chris.

"We have specially prepared rooms to help you get in the mood," Dr. Slate assured Chris before leading him into a room that was smaller than most. It only had a single bed and a nightstand upon which several pornographic magazines were sitting. "When you are finished, just press this button here, and I'll return to take the sample."

After pointing out a button near the bed, Dr. Slate left the room. Chris watched the door close behind the man. Then he sighed and wandered over to the bed. He sat down, grabbed the first magazine on top, and flipped through it. There were a number of naked catgirls in all kinds of erotic poses, and many of them were quite pretty… but Chris just couldn't get it up. He didn't know if it was because these catgirls couldn't compare to his catgirls, or if it was because Kuro, Elsa, and Silva had drained him dry this morning, but either way, he didn't think his dick would be getting hard again for a while.

"Well, this sucks," he muttered with a sigh before looking up at the ceiling. "I wonder how Kuro's and Silva's interview is going?"

Silva stared at the small restaurant, her heart thudding in her chest. It didn't look like much. It was a small building attached small strip with several other businesses. The brown walls had stone running through the center. An overhang was held up by a series of evenly intervaled support beams that looked like they probably went through the whole building. Meanwhile, sitting atop the gabled roof above the entrance was the restaurant's name: *Italianissimo Trattoria.*

Her heart felt like distant thunder. A cold sweat had broken out on her skin.

"Are you okay?" asked Kuro, placing a hand on Silva's shoulder.

Silva swallowed. "I… I am fine."

She wasn't quite fine. She was scared. Going out like this, doing something she'd never done before like this, it was frightening. But Silva didn't want to be the kind of catgirl who couldn't take care of herself. She also didn't want to be a burden on Chris. This was her chance to prove, both to herself and to Chris, that she could also be an independent person, that she wasn't with Chris because she needed him, but because she simply wanted to remain by his side.

Breathe in. Breathe out. Silva closed her eyes and took several deep breaths to calm herself down before she and Kuro entered the building.

The inside of the restaurant was rather muted. The tanned walls had picture frames and racks filled with wine bottles for decoration. A few small lamps hung from the ceiling. As she wandered between square and rectangular tables covered in white clothes, Silva glanced at the few people who were eating there. It was still fairly early—12:30 pm—and a work day, so there weren't a lot of patrons, just a few older men and women who were probably retired.

"Welcome," a young woman with blonde hair fixed into a bun greeted them with a smile. "Can I get you two a seat?"

"Um… actually…" Silva started, but her fear

caused her throat to close. Before she could panic, Kuro placed a hand on her shoulder, which helped settle her nerves. She continued talking. "We're here to be interviewed. Um, I'm here for the Commis Chef position, and Kuro is here to interview for a position as a waitress."

"Oh! You must be Silva!" the woman said, eyes widening as she looked her up and down. A slight change filled the woman's eyes like she was suddenly incredulous about something, but she quickly went back to smiling. "I was informed that you would be coming in for an interview with our head chef. And Kuro…" Finally, the woman glanced at Kuro, who towered over her like a goliath towered over an ant. She gulped. "Er, we have also been informed that you would be coming as well. Uh… our manager said he'll be interviewing you."

"Good. I hope that means Silva and I can get these interviews out of the way quickly," Kuro said with her arms crossed.

"R-right." The woman shrank away from Kuro. "A-anyway, please follow me, you two."

Silva and Kuro followed the woman, who soon introduced herself as Stephanie Dollan. She seemed personable enough as she spoke. However, the way she kept far from Kuro was quite telling.

She guided them through a door near the back, which led to both the kitchen and an office. It was the office she went to first. Knocking on the door before opening it, she peered inside and called out to whoever was on the other side of the door.

"Excuse me, Manager? Silva and Kuro have arrived," Stephanie said.

"Oh, good. Send them in," a voice came from the other side.

"Go on in," Stephanie told them before scurrying off in a hurry.

Kuro scowled at that, no doubt because the woman's hurried pace was due to her, but she plastered on a fake smile as she and Silva walked into the manager's office.

The manager's office wasn't very large, but Silva was certain the small size was due to the massive desk and filing cabinet that took up a good deal of space. Sitting behind the desk was an older man with gray hair, a trimmed goatee that gave him a somewhat refined appearance, and a business suit covering his body. He looked up when they entered, eyeing Silva for a brief moment before nearly gawking at Kuro. Unlike Stephanie, he mastered his surprise much better.

"You two are Silva and Kuro?" he asked,

standing to his feet.

"U-um, yes sir," Silva said, bowing slightly. "I'm Kuro and this is Silva—no, wait. I'm Silva and this is Kuro. It's very nice to make your acquaintance."

"You seem quite nervous," the manager said with a smile. "Relax. There is no need to be so afraid. My name is Alberto Tortellini. I'm the co-owner of this establishment. My job is managing our account and hiring on more hands, though all chef positions are handled by my younger brother."

"A pleasure," Kuro said, extending her hand. To his credit, Alberto did not pull away as he reached out and took her hand, though he did grunt at how firm her shake was.

"Anyway, Silva, let me call in my younger brother for you," Alberto said after shaking her hand next. Silva considered it a personal victory that she did not pull away from him. So far, the only man she had willingly touched was Chris.

"Th-thank you."

Alberto did indeed call in his younger brother, who seemed quite a few years younger than him. He had a head of sandy blond hair, light blue eyes, and didn't look much older than maybe his early thirties. Unlike his older brother, this man wore the white outfit of a chef. He even had one of those cool chef hats Silva had always admired when she watched her cooking channels.

"My name is Alphonse Tortellini," the man introduced himself, eyeing Silva with a frown. "Are you the one who applied for the Commis Chef position?"

"Yes… that's me." Silva did her best not to shrink underneath his gaze.

"Brother, are you sure this girl even knows how to cook? She doesn't look like much."

Silva froze. D-did this man just question her cooking skills without even seeing them? An unusual feeling permeated her being, white-hot and blazing like the fire of an old-school stone oven. She'd never felt this burning red inferno before, so it took her a moment to understand that the emotion she felt was anger.

She was angry.

How dare this man question her cooking when he hadn't even seen her in action yet.

"Don't judge someone based on their appearance," Silva said, speaking out before Alberto could say anything. The two brothers looked at her. Kuro did too, but her expression was an astonished gawk, as if she couldn't believe Silva had just spoken out like that. However, she was on a roll. "I know my way around a kitchen, so before you dismiss me, why don't you at least judge whether or not I'm fit for the position based on my skills instead of my looks?"

Alberto and Alphonse were silent for a good while. They glanced at each other, then looked at Kuro. When they saw her astonished expression, their eyes went back to Silva, who was staring at them with an unusual fire burning in her belly. Finally, Alphonse chuckled.

"This girl has got a fire in her," he said. "All right. I'll see how skilled you are in the kitchen. If you can impress me enough, I'll give you the position. However, if you fail to wow me with your skills, don't expect me to give you any handouts."

"That's fine," Silva said.

"Then follow me."

Leaving the utterly shocked Kuro behind, Silva left with Alphonse as he led her into the kitchen, which was a lot larger than the one in Chris's apartment. There were two long tables in the center and more counters and stoves located against the walls. Everything was made of gleaming steel and polished to a shine. Three people in the white uniforms of chefs looked like they were preparing for the day, but they all paused when Alphonse and Silva walked in.

Their eyes turned to Silva, who suddenly forgot

her anger in the face of so many strangers. A shudder ran through her, though she tried to hide it.

"Everyone, this is Silva," Alphonse said. "She's going to be taking a small test to see if she's fit for a position as a Commis Chef at our restaurant. I need you to clear out a section of the food prep table."

While the three chefs didn't look like they were thrilled by the idea of clearing out a section for her, the way their eyes lit up when they landed on her caused Silva to feel a small thrill run down her spine. She didn't like how some of them ran their eyes up and down her body. Even so, she did her best not to say anything. She understood that this was something she'd have to get used to. So long as they just looked… she supposed it was fine.

"All right." Alphonse turned to her as the chefs under him cleared a section of the second island table for her. "I'm going to give you a recipe from our menu. You are to follow the recipe's instructions to the best of your abilities and create the dish I've selected. I'll be evaluating you based on the appearance, taste, and speed of your cooking. Your performance will ultimately decide whether or not I hire you on as a Commis Chef."

"Yes, sir," Silva said, trying to sound determined. She was worried, her mind plagued with doubt about her abilities, but she couldn't let that stop her now that she had come all this way.

The dish she was given was called Mafalde Ai Profumi de Bosco. That made it sound complicated and foreign, but it was actually a mafalde pasta sautéed with wild mushrooms, ripe cherry tomatoes, and garlic sauce, drizzled with truffle oil.

Silva rolled up the sleeves of her shoulder-less sweater and stood before the island table, where she was to prepare her meal. She read over the instructions. Nodding once, she quickly got to work.

The ingredients had already been given to her, but she had to prep them, meaning she needed to wash, cut, and do everything else herself. She started on the porcini, a wild mushroom that would be used in this dish. She didn't bother measuring how much she used as she added them into a small bowl of boiling water. Those would need to soak for thirty minutes, so she got started on the next part, which was bringing five quarts of salted water to a boil for the pasta.

Preparing a meal with multiple steps like this meant she had to multitask. While the water for the mushrooms and pasta was boiling, she heated a heavy skillet, which was where she would make the sauce once the mushrooms were done boiling.

As she worked, she could feel the eyes of Alphonse and the other chefs on her, but at the moment they felt very distant. She was cooking. Outside of spending time with Chris, Kuro, and Elsa, this was her absolute favorite activity. Completely blocking out the stares came surprisingly easy now that she was in her zone.

Silva completely lost track of time while she cooked. However, it couldn't have been more than maybe forty-five minutes since she started. She eventually finished cooking the dish, which she served on a white plate and presented it so it looked exactly like the meal in the image she'd been given. Turning to Alphonse, Silva was prepared to present it to the man, but she froze when she noticed everyone staring at her.

"Um… is something wrong?" she asked.

"No…" Alphonse shook his head. "Let me see your dish."

"Yes, sir…"

Silva set the plate on the counter before Alphonse, who studied the dish with a studious and scrutinizing gaze. He stroked his chin in thoughtful silence for a moment before speaking.

"The dish is presented just like it should be. The smell…" he leaned in closer and took a gentle whiff before nodding. "It smells exactly as it should. Now for the taste…" He took a fork and twirled some of the pasta around it before leaning placing it inside of his mouth. Silva held her breath as the man chewed. "This is…" His eyes widened before he turned his astonished gaze on Silva, whose ears pointed straight up under his intense stare.

"Er… is it, um, good?" she asked.

"My dear," Alphonse breathed out as if he was expelling all the shock in his heart. "I have tasted the dishes of hundreds of chefs seeking a position here, and never in my life have I tasted a dish that was perfectly cooked on the first try by an untested chef."

It took a moment before Silva registered the words, but when she did, her own eyes widened.

"Then does that mean…?"

"It means you have the position," Alphonse said with a nod. "Congratulations, I'm hiring you on as our new Commis Chef."

***

Chris was exhausted when he returned home at around 3:00 pm that afternoon. It had taken him nearly an hour to get hard, and after he finally gave Dr. Slate his sperm sample, the man had stared at him with this inscrutable look that caused his embarrassment to spike. The doctor had clearly been questioning his ability to perform in bed. That had not been fun. Not at all.

Fortunately, he still passed.

The entire assessment had taken around four hours to complete, but Chris had fortunately passed every test—even the sperm sample test—with flying colors. Now he was legally capable of having catpanions. He could even apply to become a Breeder if that was what he wanted, though Chris didn't need any more catgirls. Three was enough for him.

"I'm home," he said, entering his apartment with a tired sigh. He closed and locked the door, slipped off his shoes, then looked up when he heard pounding feet coming closer.

"Chris!"

"What the—?!"

Chris barely had time to scream before Silva leapt on him, her mouth closing around his, her legs and arms wrapping him. A groan escaped his mouth as she clung to him. But just because he was shocked didn't mean he didn't respond. He quickly placed his hands underneath Silva's butt to keep her from falling as the catgirl released a purr deep within her throat. When she pulled back after ravishing his mouth, he got a glimpse of her radiant smile.

"I got the position!" she exclaimed. "I'm a Commis Chef now!"

Despite how tired he was, Chris still gave her a joyful smile. "That's great." He kissed her again, and Silva practically melted. "Congratulations." Another kiss. "I. Am. So. Proud. Of. You." Each word was accentuated by another kiss, which Silva greedily accepted.

As the two of them kissed, Kuro and Elsa wandered up to them.

"Nya ha ha! Don't hog him all to yourself!" Elsa said. "I also did a good job today! I managed to finish all the beta testing for this new program and even created two extra lines of code to enhance its performance! I deserve some praise too!"

"And I got the waitress job," Kuro added, arms crossed. "I don't need praise, but the least you can do is recognize the effort I put into getting a job I'm not equipped for."

Silva finally let go of Chris, who could properly congratulate both Elsa and Kuro. While Elsa soaked up his praise like a sponge, Kuro only blushed a little and turned her head. He was certain she didn't do well with praise for something like this. The strong woman was a warrior through and through. This whole getting a job business was new territory for her.

"So, what should we do to celebrate?" asked Chris.

When Elsa, Kuro, and Silva glanced at each other and smiled, Chris felt an unusual throbbing in his lower region. At the same time, a shiver went down his spine.

"I know exactly how we can celebrate," Kuro said, licking her lips. Silva and Elsa nodded as their gazes went straight to his crotch.

"Yeah… how about we go out for pizza instead," Chris tried. When they just shook their heads, his shoulders slumped. "I figured as much."

It looked like he was going to have a long night.

A really long night.

chapter 8

WITH THE ADVENT OF Elsa, Kuro, and Silva working, the dynamics of their relationship changed. Because Silva and Kuro sometimes worked later at night, Silva wasn't always around to cook meals, which meant Chris cooked the meals during those nights. Sometimes Silva would arrive so late that Elsa had already gone to sleep. Chris would always stay up during those nights, and Kuro waited for Silva to walk her home even if she got off her shift earlier than her silver-haired companion.

While the girls getting jobs added a bit of work to his load, it also lightened the financial burden on him, which Chris was truly thankful for. Silva and Kuro didn't get their paycheck during their first week of work. However, Elsa got paid upfront for her work. He still wasn't sure of exactly what her work entailed, but he nearly had a heart attack when Elsa showed him the $6,500 in her bank account, which she had earned from a single job. It was kind of ridiculous. It even made him feel like he was in the wrong industry.

"Nya ha ha! I told you I could be helpful," Elsa said with an upbeat smile as she sat on the couch in front of Chris, who was combing her long hair. She closed her eyes and released a soft purr. "Aren't I the best?"

"You really are," Chris said as he continued to deftly moving the brush along her hair. Elsa's hair was incredibly silky and soft, but it was also prone to getting tangled if she wasn't careful. "I'm really impressed."

He meant it too. Chris knew Elsa did some work for his mom, but he never realized she'd gained so many connections. All she had to do was tell people she was looking for work and dozens of potential employees emailed her with work. The pay was also good, and Elsa was a diligent worker. She could sometimes stay on the couch, typing away at her computer for hours. It was actually a little concerning because he discovered she would sometimes forget to eat lunch.

"This is nice," Elsa began after another moment of silence.

"Excuse me?"

"This." Elsa gestured to what he was doing. "When we were younger, you would always comb my hair like this."

"I did, didn't I?"

"Yup." Elsa looked down at her toes, which she wiggled against the carpet. "I still remember the first time you tried combing my hair. Do you remember? You were so bad at it. My hair was tangled in all these knots, and you started combing from the top. It hurt so bad I thought my scalp would be torn off."

"T-that was because I was young and never combed a girl's hair before." Chris was pleased when he only stuttered a little.

"I know." Elsa smiled. "After that, Momma showed you how to comb a girl's hair properly. You've been an expert ever since." Elsa almost leaned back as Chris finally reached her scalp, gently gliding the comb through it. "These days I won't even let anyone besides you comb my hair."

"That's actually kind of embarrassing to hear, but it does make me happy," Chris admitted.

"Mm. Me too."

The room became quiet again as Chris finally finished combing her hair. It had taken about one hour. When he glanced at the clock, he saw that it was nearly 4:00 pm. It wasn't time to get started on dinner yet.

"Kuro and Silva won't be home for another four hours," he said after a moment. "And I'm all done with my homework." He glanced at Elsa. "What should we do in the meantime?"

"Monster Hunter!" Elsa shouted with a grin.

Before Chris had time to agree or disagree, she had hopped off the couch and rushed over to the TV stand. Her blonde tail was wagging like a dog's as she grabbed a pair of PSPs and came back to the couch. At the moment, Elsa was wearing a simple tank top and pink booty shorts. When she moved, Chris caught a glimpse of her flat soft belly. Then she was sitting down, handing him one of the PSPs, and moving to the opposite side of the couch.

"It's been a long time since we played together," Elsa said. "I normally play with Silva, but she's more into anime and cooking channels than video games."

Chris nodded as he turned on the console and booted up the start-up screen. It had been a long time since he'd played, but it looked like his old character was still there. His name was Melopan… which was an admittedly bad name he created because of a YouTuber he used to watch when he was younger. His character was a male with blond hair and green eyes. He wore white fatalis armor and he dual-wielded a pair of Azure Dual Swords. They weren't the best in the game, but they were decent weapons.

"You ready?" asked Elsa.

"Yes," Chris said. "Whenever you are."

"Nya ha ha! Then let's do this!"

Chris and Elsa started the game. *Monster Hunter Freedom Unite* didn't support local or online co-op, but it was possible to adventure with up to three players using the wireless Ad-Hoc connection. When they were younger, Chris and Elsa had done this a lot. Sometimes his brother would join them, but he was more of a jock than a gamer and spent most of his time playing sports or going outdoors.

As they played, Chris looked up from his screen to see Elsa sitting with her back against the armrest and one leg off the couch. Her shorts were already on the short side, and when she spread her legs like she was, he could see her white lace panties peeking out. Her soft white skin was complemented by the equally white lace. It looked like she had chosen to wear something sexy.

He tried to ignore the way his dick twitched and keep playing, but several minutes of on and off looking caused Elsa to notice. With a cat-like grin, she reached out with her right leg and placed her foot against his cock, rubbing her soft toes along his hard shaft through their clothing.

"Do you like the view?" she asked. "Nya ha ha. I wore this outfit specifically so you would notice me."

"I-I always notice you," Chris admitted with a slight stutter.

"Is that so? I'm glad to hear it."

Elsa smiled widely as she continued rubbing his dick with her toes. The feeling was slightly muted through his clothing, but perhaps because this was something new, the sensations seemed stronger. It felt like an electric discharge was racing through his dick and straight into his brain.

It was impossible for Chris to concentrate on playing now, but Elsa didn't seem to mind as they both turned off their consoles. Chris then removed his pants. When his dick sprang free, Elsa smiled widely and used both of her feet to stimulate his dick. She trapped his cock between the soles of her feet and went from his shaft all the way to his head, then repeated the process.

"How... does that feel?" asked Elsa.

"G-good. I didn't think... didn't think something like this... would feel so good."

"That makes me happy. I've always been curious and wanted to try this."

As she continued to give him a footjob, Elsa lifted her tank top over her breasts. She wasn't wearing a bra today, perhaps because she had been expecting this to happen, so she didn't need to remove anything in order to fondle herself. One hand went to her breasts, while the other slipped underneath her shorts and panties.

Chris groaned as Elsa pinched and played with her nipple and fingered herself. The sight of Elsa plunging two of her delicate fingers into the depths of her cunt was more erotic than many things he'd seen. Juices flowed between her fingers as a light sweat broke out on her skin. Elsa's breathing had grown increasingly heavy alongside his own, and loud purrs soon echoed from her throat as she began rubbing her clit with her thumb.

Unable to handle any more stimulation, Chris grabbed Elsa's small feet and began using them to jerk off. It was... unbelievable. He'd never really considered himself a fetish kind of guy. Outside of standard fetishes like titjobs and whatnot, he really preferred normal sex, but he couldn't lie and say there wasn't something hot about this. Elsa's feet were softer than his hands. Her small toes curled around his dick. And the sight before him, of Elsa biting her lips, eyes closed as she played with her tits and masturbated, creating a visual stimulation that tipped him over the edge.

Chris grunted as he shot several loads of cum, which spurted out and splattered against Elsa's feet and calves. At the same time, Elsa released a loud

"Nya!" as her own body twitched and shuddered. She slumped against the couch seconds later.

"Let me get something to clean you off with," Chris murmured as he stood up and stumbled toward the cabinet in his bathroom. He soaked a washcloth in water, came back, and began wiping his cum off her feet and calves. Elsa watched him with a half-lidded smile.

"Nya ha… you're hard again. Are my feet really that sexy?"

"Everything about you is sexy," Chris admitted.

His words were the right ones. Elsa's eyes brightened.

As he finished cleaning her off, Elsa gripped the hem of her shorts and panties, then slid them off her legs. Her pussy was puffy from her own self-gratification. As she laid back down, Elsa placed one foot against the floor and rested the other against the head of the couch. She reached down and spread her pussy apart, revealing the soft pink interior.

"Chris… I'm not satisfied yet," she said to him, her eyes vibrant and sparkling as the evening glow of the sun hit her. "I need something to fill me up."

"It would be a shame if you weren't fully satisfied," Chris said as he moved between her legs and placed his once more erect cock against her lower stomach.

"It would," Elsa agreed. "So please… fill me up."

Chris smiled as he gripped her legs, placing them over his shoulders before smoothly inserting his cock into her cunt. Elsa purred as he moved slowly, bottoming out inside of her, then released a soft "nya" as he retracted his hips. Chris's breathing stuttered as her warm, wet, and squishy insides rubbed against him, sending jolts of electric pleasure straight to his brain. However, he soon worked up a nice pace.

"Hyk! Nya! Ah! Nya!"

As he increased the pace of his thrusts, Elsa's tits began bouncing all over the place as she released a series of unusual but erotic moans. Chris placed his hands on the back of her knees. Now that he was thinking about it, the back of the knee didn't technically have a name. Maybe he should call them kneepits? Shaking his head, he dispelled that thought and, as he continued to thrust into her, pressed her legs down until her knees were resting against her chest.

"Chris! Chris! I love you! Nya! I-I love you so much!"

"I… love you… too."

Chris grunted as he continued to pound into her. He felt his balls tightening and pressure building in his lower stomach. He wasn't going to last much longer.

An odd idea came to him then, and Chris acted on it, taking one of Elsa's feet and sucking her big toe into his mouth. Elsa, to his surprise, released an intense scream as her back arched. Was this a weakness? He had noticed how horny she got when she gave him a footjob. He'd thought she was just getting aroused by what was happening, but maybe her feet were an erogenous zone.

Testing this theory, Chris began sucking on each individual toe, swirling his tongue around them and even licking the soles of her feet. Elsa's mouth opened wide as she moaned. Drool leaked from her lips and her eyes rolled into the back of her head. Her entire body went into a series of shudders before her cunt tightened around his cock, yet the juices flowing out of her increased. At that moment, Chris felt his own end coming and thrust himself as far into her as he could go.

"Nya!!!"

Elsa unleashed a loud cry as he released his seed inside of her. His world went white as pleasure overrode his ability to think, then he came back down to find Elsa, still lying on the couch. Her left arm and leg were hanging off the couch now, but her right leg was resting on his shoulder. He removed it, setting it down, and leaned forward until her breasts were pressed against his chest.

"Ha… ha… Chris…"

Chris leaned down the rest of the way and kissed Elsa on the lips, which made the girl greedily respond to his affection by wrapping her arms around his neck and kissing back. When he moved back, it was only a few inches. Elsa kept her arms locked around him and rubbed their noses together.

"More… I want more," she demanded.

Chris rolled his eyes. "I have to get started on dinner."

Elsa pouted. "But… but…"

"Not buts. You want to eat, don't you? Besides, you girls are running me ragged."

Elsa, Kuro, and Silva had fairly high libidos. Out of the three of them, he would say the one who wanted sex the most was Silva, surprisingly, while Kuro came to him the least. Elsa was somewhere in between the two. That said, even if one of them had a higher libido than the others, all three were still fairly voracious and wanted sex regularly.

Chris was just one guy, and while he did pride himself on being able to please his catpanions in and out of the bed, it didn't change the fact that any person was going to have a hard time keeping up with multiple catgirls.

"F-fine…" Elsa sighed as she released her grip on his neck.

Chris grinned as he gave her one final kiss began standing up and heading toward the bathroom. He at least wanted to take a quick shower and get dressed before cooking dinner.

***

Silva put the finishing touches on the Spaghetti Carbonara she'd been making before taking a step back. A smile split her face as she admired her work. It looked perfect, just like it was supposed to. With her smile growing, she used a testing fork to check the flavor, twirling a small bit of the pasta around the fork and sticking it into her mouth.

"Mmmmm…" Silva released a low, satisfied moan. "It's purrfect."

It looked right, tasted great, and was ready to be served. Silva set her fork down and nodded once to herself.

"You've gotten pretty good," someone complimented from her left.

Silva stiffened only a little at the voice that was practically speaking into her ear. She stepped back a little and turned around, looking at the young man with dark hair, dark eyes, and pale skin. He wore the same white chef's uniform as her. While their uniforms might have looked the same, this man was the Sous Chef of Italianissimo Trattoria. That meant he was ranked higher than her on the cooking ladder.

"Thank you, Mr. Valentine."

Alessio Valentine was the second in command of all the chefs and the person who Alphonse had put in charge of teaching her. Silva didn't think he was a bad person, but he also made her uncomfortable. He'd invade her personal space, whisper in her ear, and sometimes place a hand on her shoulder. One time he had even placed his hand on her lower back. She wanted to tell him not to, but he was also her boss. Silva didn't want to risk her job when he hadn't really done anything.

"Not at all." Mr. Valentine smiled at her. "You do good work. I'm just being honest."

"Thank you."

He moved off again, snapping orders to several of the other chefs, and Silva quietly breathed a sigh of relief as she got back to work.

The rest of her shift went by smoothly enough. As a Commis Chef, her job was mostly assisting the other chefs in the kitchen. She helped prepare the ingredients and do any tasks the chef de partie needed assistance with. This meant she was usually moving around the kitchen and helping out with whatever she could, which included cutting vegetables, peeling vegetables, preparing meat, making sauces, and so on. It was hard work, but Silva also thought it was rewarding.

Her shift eventually came to an end, and Silva moved into the locker room and changed out of her chef uniform. She wore her normal clothes beneath her chef outfit. All she had to do was remove her uniform and hang it up in her locker. After which, she walked down the hall toward the back door.

She paused when she saw Mr. Valentine standing there.

"Hey there," he greeted.

"Um… hi." Silva tried to offer him a polite smile as she made to walk around him, but he stepped in front of her.

"Whoa there," he said. "Sorry, but I actually wanted to talk with you a bit."

"Um… but I'm not on my shift," Silva said. She tried to keep her breathing calm and even. They were in a workplace, so he wouldn't do anything to her… right?

"I know, but it won't take long." Despite his assurance, Silva really wasn't sure she wanted to speak with him. He continued anyway. "Listen, the weekend is coming up, and I wanted to ask if you could stop by my place? I've got some new dishes I've prepared. I'm going to try and present them to the Head Chef, but I need someone who can taste test them for me. Would you be willing?"

Silva felt a moment of turmoil. Truth be told, she didn't want to be alone with this man. Even if he wasn't a bad person, he just made her uncomfortable. He didn't seem to have any concept of personal space. The last thing she wanted was this guy getting close to her when there was no one else around.

"Um…"

As Silva struggled with how she could turn him down without making him angry, someone else walked into the hallway.

"Silva!" Kuro said in a loud voice. The dark-skinned beauty with the bearing of a warrior walked up to her with a grin. Meanwhile, Mr. Valentine took a step back as he eyed the woman like prey fearfully stared at a predator. If Kuro noticed, she didn't let on. "Looks like you're off your shift too. Let's head home."

"Right!" Silva tried not to let the relief show on her face as she smiled at Mr. Valentine. "I'll see you later."

"Ah, er, uh, wait a minute—"

Mr. Valentine stretched out a hand as if to stop her from leaving, but Kuro and Silva were already out the door. They traveled out of the alley and began walking down the street. The air was mild but not cold. It felt nice. As they walked, Silva sighed again and looked at Kuro.

"Thanks for helping me out back there," she said.

"It's not a problem," Kuro replied. Then she scowled. "That man is always getting too close to you for my liking. You should tell him to stop."

"But… he hasn't really done anything," Silva admitted.

"That… is true, but even so…" Kuro's scowl grew a little more.

A smile appeared on Silva's face again. She was grateful for her friend's presence. While she'd been reluctant to have Kuro working the same job because she wanted to prove that she could be strong and independent, Silva now realized how nice it was to have someone who could watch after her. Had she been alone, there was a good chance she would have caved to Mr. Valentine's request, which she didn't want.

"You should at least tell Chris," Kuro said at last.

Silva thought about that for a moment, then reluctantly agreed. "I don't want to bother him, but maybe I should. Okay. I'll tell him when we get home."

"Good."

They walked the rest of the way home in silence, traveled up the stairs, and entered Chris's apartment. When they arrived, it was to find Chris sitting at the dinner table with two plates of baked salmon sitting at the spots where Kuro and Silva traditionally sat during dinner. Silva took several surprised sniffs of the air as the scent from Chris's cooking wafted to them. It smelled delicious.

"Evening, you two." Chris smiled at them as they slipped off their shoes and walked in. "How was work?"

"It was a lot of fun," Kuro said with a grin. "I get to scare the customers with my size. Oddly enough, some of the kids who show up seem to love me."

"You are awfully lovable," Chris said with a grin. "Just like a big teddy bear."

Kuro scowled, but there was no heat to it. "This teddy bear could crush your head between her thighs."

"That would be quite the way to go," Chris joked.

As Kuro and Chris shared a chuckle, Silva sat down at her seat and looked at the food. Now that she had learned so much about cooking, she could tell the fish was a little overcooked, but it still flaked easily when she took a fork to it. She could also tell from the color that this salmon had been baked in tin foil. It had been lightly seasoned with salt and pepper, then lemon slices, dill, and capers had been added. It wasn't the best meal ever, but when Silva placed a small bite inside of her mouth and chewed, her entire body thrummed with pleasure.

She loved Chris's cooking.

Even if her cooking was better.

"Silva?" Chris suddenly said as Kuro began to eat.

"Yes?" Silva looked up from her meal.

"Are you okay? You seem distracted."

"I'm…" Silva was about to say "I'm fine" as an automatic response, then she paused. "To be honest, I'm having a bit of trouble with one of my co-workers."

Silva went on to explain how the Sous Chef, Alessio Valentine, sometimes got closer to her than she was comfortable with, how he would place his hands on her shoulders, or how he'd whisper in her ear. She told him that she didn't like it, but she couldn't say anything since he hadn't really done anything.

"I'm not sure what to do," Silva admitted.

"Hmm…" Chris rubbed his chin in thought.

"Chris?" Silva asked.

"It's nothing," Chris said. "Anyway, about this guy, just remain cautious. It doesn't sound like he's trying to make you uncomfortable, but if he does something more, be sure to tell him how you feel. It could just be that he's trying to make you feel at ease and doesn't realize he's doing the opposite, or he could have a thing for you and wants to try and deepen his relationship with you."

Silva shuddered at the idea of Mr. Valentine having a thing for her, but she nodded in agreement with Chris's assessment. She would do what he said. Of course, she hoped nothing of the sort would happen.

The next day at work, Silva did the same thing she always did. She helped the other chefs prepare their ingredients, worked as hard as she could, and tried to ignore Mr. Valentine's behavior. It wasn't easy, but it wasn't exactly hard either. The other two chefs and Alphonse were easy to get along with. They were friendly and open without getting in her personal space, and they always thanked her for working hard.

After her shift ended, Silva took off her uniform, hung it up, and walked out back, where she waited for Kuro. As she was waiting, the backdoor opened and Silva turned, expecting to see her companion. Her spine stiffened when she saw that it was Mr. Valentine.

"Oh, Mr. Valentine." She offered him a polite

smile. "Don't you still have work?"

"I'm on break," Mr. Valentine said as he walked over to her. He was smiling like usual. It was the same friendly smile as always, but that was what made her so uncomfortable.

"And you don't want to take your break inside?" Silva asked, curious.

"Naw. It's too stuffy inside," Mr. Valentine admitted.

"Oh…"

Silva wasn't sure what to say, so she opted to say nothing and instead wait for Kuro. A frown marred her face, though, as she wondered how much longer her friend would take. Kuro got off work later than her today since she was closing. That meant she might have to wait here for longer than necessary.

Alone with Mr. Valentine.

"Say…" Mr. Valentine began.

"Y-yes?" Silva squeaked.

"Do you not like me?" he asked.

"Uh… what gave you that idea?" asked Silva, carefully keeping her emotions hidden.

"It's just that you seem jumpy whenever I'm near you."

So he had noticed. Silva had thought she'd done a good job of masking her discomfort, but Mr.

Valentine was more perceptive than she assumed, or maybe she was just worse at hiding her emotions than she thought. Since it looked like he had seen through her, there was no point in hiding it.

"Um… to be honest, I get uncomfortable whenever you touch my shoulders or whisper in my ear. You also get too close. I'm not really comfortable when you invade my personal space."

"Ah. I see." He rubbed the back of his neck as his smile turned apologetic. "I'm sorry about that. I wasn't sure how to treat you because you're a catgirl and I haven't had much experience dealing with catgirls, so I tried to be more familial. I come from a big Italian family, and we're all pretty, how do you say, touchy-feely? We share hugs and kisses and act very close. I thought it would make you more comfortable, but I guess it did the opposite. I'll remember this from now on and be a bit more respectful of your boundaries."

"Th-thank you very much."

Silva couldn't quite contain her sigh of relief. She'd been worrying this whole time, but it seemed like maybe she had been working herself up for nothing.

"That said," Mr. Valentine continued, "I do want you to know that I am interested in you—as more than just a co-worker, I mean. You're cute and hardworking, so I was hoping I could get to know you better.”

“I’m very sorry,” Silva said, bowing to the man. “But I’m actually a registered catpanion.”

“I should have figured as much.” Mr. Valentine released a sigh as he scratched his head. “A girl like you definitely wouldn’t be single. Whoever your partner is, he’s one lucky guy.”

“Thank you for saying so, but I often feel like I’m the lucky one,” Silva said.

“Is that right?”

Another silence elapsed between them, but it wasn’t quite as uncomfortable as before. Silva now realized that Mr. Valentine hadn’t been making her wary of him on purpose, but had merely been trying, in his own way, to make her feel welcome. It helped settle her nerves.

“Silva!” a familiar voice suddenly called her name.

It wasn’t Kuro.

“Chris?” Silva blinked as Chris walked up to her. He was dressed in jeans, a black T-shirt, and a slim jacket that fit his muscular frame well. His tousled brown hair was a bit messier than usual, making it look like he’d run to get here. She admired his broad shoulders and strong arms and chest for a moment before realizing something. “What are you doing here?"

"My kickboxing ran a bit late," Chris admitted with a shrug. "Since I knew you got off at this time, I figured I would come by and walk home with you."

Silva could not quite contain her smile as Chris stopped in front of her and leaned down for a soft kiss. She grabbed the lapels of his jacket as she tilted her head slightly and stood on her tiptoes to better kiss him. As his taste invaded her tongue, she released a soft sigh, relishing in the feel of his lips, the scent of his body, and the strong hands resting lightly on her hips. The kiss didn't last long. It was too short actually, but she finally remembered there was someone else with them.

"You must be Silva's partner," Mr. Valentine said with a slight smile.

"Yes, I am," Chris responded with a polite nod. "I'm guessing you're a co-worker of hers."

"My name is Alessio Valentine," he said as he extended a hand. "Well, Valentino is my actual last name, but people have been calling me Valentine since I was in middle school and it just kind of stuck."

"Chris Redford." Chris reached out and shook the man's hand. "It's nice to meet you."

"You've got a firm grip," Mr. Valentine said. "You must be incredibly happy with your catpanion.

Silva works hard and has a lot of talent for cooking. Be sure to treat her well."

"I will," Chris assured the man.

Mr. Valentine said goodbye to Silva as he traveled back inside, leaving the two of them alone. Chris reached out and grabbed her hand. Silva laced her fingers through his hand and looked at him in curiosity.

"Did you come here because of what I said last night?" she asked.

"I was being honest when I said kickboxing ran late," Chris said, then looked down at her with a smile. "But when one of my catpanions tells me that one of her co-workers is making her uncomfortable… well, I can't help but get worried and want to at least check things out, you know?"

A warm feeling encapsulated Silva's heart, spreading out to the rest of her body. She leaned into him, enjoying the warmth his body emitted. It wasn't just a physical warmth either. Chris was such a warm person, kind and thoughtful, that she felt like she was falling in love with him all over again.

"Thank you, Chris."

"You're welcome."

After that night, whenever Silva worked, Mr. Valentine made sure to keep a respectful distance, though he was still very friendly and helpful.

chapter 9

THE DAYS PASSED by. Elsa continued to work her freelance jobs as a programmer and even began doing web design. Meanwhile, Kuro became oddly popular as a waitress at Italianissimo Trattoria. Chris had even heard several people at his college talk about the "dark-skinned waitress with ridiculous muscles" when he was walking through the campus. He had actually eaten there on a number of occasions—mostly to see how she and Silva were doing—and everyone, from the staff to the guests, seemed to love her.

However, out of all his catgirls, the one who shone the most was Silva.

His first catpanion had really come into herself. Chris still remembered their first few days cohabitating. Back then, Silva could barely stand to go outside, and when she did go outside, she was afraid of everyone who wasn't him. Now Silva was working as a Commis Chef and had even confronted someone who made her uncomfortable and managed to work out the misunderstanding all by herself.

Chris had never been more proud of her.

Each day went by, and it wasn't long before the final examinations for the Fall Semester began. Chris was forced to buckle down and study for the finals. Some of the tests were simple, like the ones for English Composition, Anatomy and Physiology, and Quantitative Analysis. Well, he called them simple, but he meant that in a relative term. Quantitative Analysis was going to be incredibly hard since he sucked at and hated math with a passion, but it was nowhere near as difficult as creating a speech that expressed his views on why harsher standards were needed for people to own a Catgirl Guardianship License.

That was why he and Anastasia had taken to staying a little later after school every day so they could practice giving each other their respective speeches. Each time they finished, the other person would critique them on things like their performance, how accurate and informative the information provided was, and whether or not they felt it would be enough to move Professor Shinomiya.

"It's not bad," Anastasia said as Chris finished giving her his speech and sat down. Despite her words, she was frowning. "Your speaking is clear and your enunciation is fine. I even agree with you on all your points. However, while your argument is compelling, I'm not so certain it's what Professor Shinomiya wants. Don't forget this class is Catgirl Biology. We study the inner workings of the body, not the psyche."

"So you think I should change my theme?" Chris asked for clarification.

"Either change your theme or change how you plan on broaching this subject." Anastasia paused and tilted her head. "For example, instead of talking about how an abusive guardian can mentally damage a catgirl, talk about how they can physically damage a catgirl via abuse. Like, say the guardian is physically abusive and damages their ability to procreate or something else."

"The mind is also an organ, you know." Chris sighed. "But I see your point. I'll make some changes so I'm discussing the physical ramifications instead of the psychological ones."

They were in the library, which was filled with a lot of other people. Sitting at a table several yards away was a mixture of men and women, all of whom had their faces buried in their notes, and Chris even saw one or two catgirls studying in the library. They were just a little to his right. It looked like they were quizzing each other. He thought he recognized one of them. It was that girl Jason had protected from those jocks.

"Now it's my turn," Anastasia stood up, clearing her throat. "Good evening, everyone. Today, I want to discuss the ramifications of unsuccessful childbirth among catgirls, and why I believe it is important to upgrade all the equipment currently being used in certified Catgirl Hospitals…"

Chris was honestly amazed as he listened to Anastasia as she spoke, citing a variety of different sources to enunciate her points. She mentioned how the current equipment being used was the same that was used for humans. However, a lot of that equipment couldn't accurately catalog all the changes happening inside of a catgirl because of the minute differences in their biology. Catgirls were like a blend of domesticated house cat and human. Their biological functions, therefore, had a mixture of the two.

"Because of these unique differences between catgirls, humans, and cats, I believe we should be focusing on creating brand new equipment made specifically for catgirls," Anastasia concluded. "That is all for my report. Thank you."

Chris softly clapped. "That was really good. I'm impressed."

"Thank you." Anastasia brushed a strand of hair

behind her left ear as she sat down. "I've been working on this day and night after our last study session. You mentioned I went too much into the equipment's specifications and didn't discuss how that equipment couldn't accurately gauge a catgirl's biological functions enough. I did that because I needed to pad my word count so I could make this last the full thirty minutes. But I know it wouldn't have earned me full marks in Professor Shinomiya's class."

Chris could only agree.

After she finished presenting her speech, they sat down and discussed what changes they needed to make. Anastasia still needed to add another paragraph or two. Her speech was five minutes short of the thirty minute presentation mark, which she needed to hit if she wanted full credit. On the other hand, Chris needed to change what he was talking about because his current speech spoke more of psychological effects than it did physical ones.

The time passed before the two of them were finished. At least for now. Chris and Anastasia eventually stood from their seats.

"I'll see you later, Chris."

"Goodbye for now, Anastasia."

They parted ways and Chris headed for the bus station, where he hopped onto a bus that took him close to his kickboxing center.

As always, the kickboxing center was busy. There were people pounding away at the punching bags, stretching on the mats, and exercising in the free weight area. The strong scent of sweat hung in the air, only partially deadened by the air fresheners placed evenly against the walls. Sadly, no amount of air fresheners could completely clean out the scent of BO when so many people came to exercise.

Chris traveled to the backroom and changed into his workout clothes. As he emerged, he found Tanner waiting for him.

"Captain," he greeted.

Tanner grinned. His dark skin had a light sheen of sweat, but he didn't seem anywhere close to being winded. He'd probably just been helping some of the other people working there.

"Hey there. I figured we'd start off with some light stretches before heading to the punching bags. I want you to work up a good sweat and limber up before we begin sparring today."

"Yes, sir."

Because Tanner believed having a routine ruined a person's physical fitness, he never had Chris do the same workout twice. Even his stretches from day to day were different. However, Chris didn't complain since he agreed with the man's assessment. His own physical prowess was proof that Tanner knew what he was doing.

"You seem to be doing well," Tanner said as he stood behind the punching back and kept it in place for Chris to hit. The dull thuds of Chris's fist pounding away at the bag echoed around them. "How's life with your harem?"

"I. Wish. You. Wouldn't. Call. Them. That." Each of Chris's words was accentuated by a thrown fist, followed by a loud cracking sound as his fist struck the punching bag. He mixed up his attacks, throwing several jabs before hitting the bag with a powerful cross or a reverse heel kick.

"If not a harem, then what should I call it?" asked Tanner.

His words brought Chris up short, though he didn't stop hitting the punching bag. Speaking in technical terms, Chris's catpanions would be considered a harem, which was defined as the women occupying a harem, or the wives (or concubines) of a polygamous man. He had never really thought about what it meant to have three catpanions in those terms. It wasn't like he was all that interested in polygamy. His only real concern was graduating college, becoming a catgirl doctor, and making sure Elsa, Kuro, and Silva were happy.

"My family," he said at last.

Tanner chuckled. "Fair enough. How is it living with your family?"

"It's good," Chris said as he threw out a one, two combination, then launched a high kick that struck the top of the punching bag. He'd become much more limber thanks to constantly working out with Kuro. "All of us have pulled together and are doing our best. We're not in any financial trouble, and thanks to the girls working, we can afford to go out on dates instead of staying at home during the weekends."

They went on dates nearly every weekend these days. Sometimes they would go out as a group and sometimes they would go on individual dates. Their last date had been one where all four of them went to Disneyland for the weekend. It had been fun, though several of the other guests staying at the same hotel had complained about the noises coming from their room.

"And it doesn't bother you that your catpanions are the ones bringing home the bacon?" Tanner asked with a teasing grin.

"Should it?" Chris fired back. "I've never been the kind of person to let this sort of thing bother me. I'm not so chauvinistic that I think a woman can't be more successful than a man." Chris released a deep sigh as the timer went off and stepped back, a smile breaking out on his face. "Besides, they told me it makes them happy that they don't have to rely on me. They're not with me because I'm the one providing for them but because being with me is what makes them happy. I honestly prefer that manner of thinking. A man who has to tie a woman down because she needs him to provide for her isn't much of a man."

"I suppose you have a point," Tanner said with a slow nod. "Anyway, let's end with our usual spar."

"Right."

Chris sparred with Tanner for twenty minutes, and while he didn't defeat the more experienced man, he wouldn't say he lost either. Sweat poured from his body in rivulets by the time they were finished. The hot shower he took to rid himself of it was heavenly, though he wished his catpanions had been with him to enjoy it.

After showering and getting dressed, Chris walked home. He cut through the alleys and eventually made his way to Memorial Park. The sight of his apartment complex peeked out over the trees. As he walked through the park, his eyes landed on the bridge where he found Silva all those months ago, causing him to stop and remember. While that moment had been horrible, it had also been a blessing.

He had met Silva because of that moment back then. Chris felt a little guilty. Silva's pain and suffering were what had brought her to him. Had she not been Markus Flint's captive, had she not run away, had she not collapsed there, had she found a better guardian, they would have never met. Silva had once told him she was glad all those things happened because it brought her to him, but a part of him wished she never had to go through what she did. Still, he couldn't lie and say he wasn't happy she was in his life.

Shaking his head, Chris made it back to his complex, reached the second floor, and entered his apartment.

"Nya ha ha ha! Did you really think you could defeat me, you pathetic sacks of shit! I am the all-powerful magical sniper girl!"

The first thing he heard was Elsa's laughter and taunting insults. The Birman catgirl was sitting with her legs crossed on the couch, controller in hand and headset on, playing what appeared to be the current hottest battle royale game on the market. It looked like she was playing Wraith, a woman who could manipulate spacetime by opening rifts in the fabric of reality. Even as he watched, Elsa opened a portal, appeared on the roof, and blasted a hole through an enemy player's head.

"Nya ha ha ha! Take that, bitches!"

Chris absently wondered if he should pose restrictions on her language as he slipped out of his shoes and placed them off to the side. Wandering further into the apartment, he found Kuro setting the dinner table. Her clothing was the same carpenter pants and sleeveless shirt she always wore. Her massive chest was being held up by a custom bra since there were no regular bras in her size.

She noticed him and flashed him a fanged grin. "Hey, hon. We figured you'd be getting home later than usual."

"Kuro. No work today?" Chris asked as he set his backpack down and came back out. He noticed Silva was cooking something in the kitchen. The tantalizing scent of braised lamb and red wine filled his nose and made his stomach gurgle.

Kuro shook her head. "Not today. I actually just got back from visiting Sister Ann's orphanage. Hey, did you hear that Calvin Lafaard is actually the reason why we were moved there?"

"I didn't," Chris said with furrowed brows.

Nodding, Kuro said, "It seems we should have gone to a catgirl-only housing complex, but Calvin Lafaard pulled some strings to have us moved into

Sister Ann's orphanage. As I understand it, his plan was not just to take the orphanage but to also claim custody of us. He wanted to train me and the other catgirls into obedient sex slaves that he planned to sell on the slave market. Not that I would have let him."

Chris nearly blew out a breath as he heard this. He didn't know where Kuro had acquired her information, but he didn't doubt that what she said was true. It actually made sense. They should have been relocated to a government-owned facility made for catgirls, but they had instead been given to a rundown orphanage owned by a nun. Someone would have had to pull some strings to make that happen. Chris wondered if whoever Calvin Lafaard had under his thumb had been fired after this debacle. He hoped so.

"I'm glad we were able to put him behind bars," Chris said.

"Me too," said Kuro, though she twitched when Elsa's "Nya ha ha ha!" overpowered her words.

Chris snorted as he wandered into the kitchen. The scents of onions, garlic, ginger, and cinnamon mixed in with the lamb were far stronger in here than outside. Silva was slowly simmering the braised lamb. It looked like she was using red wine to simmer it.

Silva was dressed in jean shorts that ended just below her butt, a simple T-shirt, and an apron. Her long silver hair had been tied into a ponytail.

He took in the scent as he moved behind Silva and wrapped his arms around her.

"Hey," he said.

Silva jerked a bit, but then relaxed and leaned into him. "Welcome home, Chris. Dinner is almost ready."

"I know." Chris chuckled as he leaned down and placed his lips against Silva's neck. She shivered and released a soft purring sound from the back of her throat as she tilted her head to grant him better access to her neck. "It smells delicious."

"Mmm. It's a new recipe I learned. You'll have to… let me know what you think," she said, her breath hitching just a bit as Chris kissed her jawline.

"I will," Chris assured her.

It didn't need to be said, but dinner that night was delicious. Silva's cooking had come a long way from where it had been. Unlike Chris, who could only follow directions when he cooked, she could now create her own dishes thanks to the knowledge and experience she gained from working in the kitchen of a restaurant. She'd reached a point where Chris was entirely certain she could go onto one of Gordon Ramsay's shows and actually earn the infamous chef's approval.

Silva, of course, blushed and denied that when he

told her. She blushed even harder when Kuro and Elsa agreed with him.

Later that night, Chris was sitting in bed with his three catpanions, a brand new laptop on his lap. It was something his catgirls had bought for him as a birthday present. This new laptop had even better hardware than his desktop.

He was changing up his speech based on the advice Anastasia had given him. Instead of focusing on the psychological effects that came from being with an abusive owner, he was adding information on how it could affect them physically. He tried to tie in the psychological effects with the physical effects since the brain was an organ. However, he had to delete entire paragraphs' worth of content as well.

Kuro and Elsa were fast asleep. Kuro's snores as she buried her face in his shoulder were loud but unobtrusive. He'd grown so used to them that he didn't think he'd be able to fall asleep without them. Meanwhile, Elsa was sprawled out across his, Kuro's, and Silva's legs, lying on her back as her pink pajama shirt rode up to reveal her stomach. He wondered if she was comfortable like that, but when he looked, he saw the girl was mumbling in her sleep and had a stupid smile on her face. He assumed she was fine.

The only person awake aside from him was Silva,

his first catgirl and the one who never went to sleep until he planned on going to sleep as well. She leaned against him as she flipped through the pages of her book. It was a manga. *Food Wars*. Chris hadn't read the manga series of that, but he had seen the anime. It was a series that mixed cooking with a battle royale style tournament and fan service, which gave it a unique flavor and made it incredibly popular—popular enough that three whole seasons had been made of it.

"Okay." Chris stretched his arms above his head, grimacing as his back and shoulders popped, then brought them back down so he could close his laptop. "I think I'm done."

"You have to deliver that speech in a few days, right?" Silva said as she placed a bookmark in her manga and closed it. "Think you'll be ready?"

"I think so," Chris said as he handed the laptop to Silva, who placed it and her manga on the nightstand next to the bed. He settled down against the pillow as Silva scooted closer and set her head on his chest. On his other side, Kuro snorted and nuzzled his shoulder with her nose. He sighed. She was drooling on him.

"I wish I could be there when you deliver it," Silva admitted as she closed her eyes.

"Me too. But don't worry. I'm sure everything

will work out."

"I know it will. You worked too hard to fail."

A soft silence permeated the room as Chris stared at the ceiling. He reached up and stroked Silva's back and Kuro's shoulder and arm. His actions earned soft purring from both of them. Had Elsa not been lying across their legs, he was sure Kuro would have thrown her leg over his body by now.

"Summer is coming up soon," Chris said. "I'm thinking we should travel to my parents and pay them a visit."

Silva opened her eyes and lifted her head from his chest. "I'm going to meet your parents?"

Chris nodded. "It's about time I introduced my catpanions to the rest of my family."

Her eyes widened, but then a gentle smile replaced it as she leaned up and kissed his cheek. "I would very much like to meet your parents."

Chris smiled as well. "I know they'll love you." He paused as the smile turned wry. "They may even love you too much."

Silva giggled at that, then settled down on his chest again. As they both closed their eyes and drifted to sleep, Chris thought about what would happen when Silva and Kuro were introduced to his family. He was sure it would be interesting.

***

The day of Chris's speech came and went. Thanks to the study sessions he had with Anastasia, Chris earned full marks on his final exams in Catgirl Biology. Sadly, while he did well in most of his other classes too, his final score in Quantitative Analysis was low enough to drop his overall grade from a 4.0 to a 3.8. That was still good, but he'd been hoping to keep his 4.0 average.

While his grades had dropped a little, Chris couldn't complain too much since it was now the beginning of summer, and that meant it was time for him, Elsa, Kuro, and Silva to leave Chula Vista and make their way to his family's house in San Jose.

Of course, this meant scrambling to get all their last-minute items packed because they hadn't prepared everything despite having several days to do it.

"Nya ha ha! C-Chris! I can't find my laptop!"

"It should be in your suitcase, shouldn't it?"

"Oh! Here it is! Nya ha ha! Thank you, Chris!"

"Damn it! Where is my flask?!"

"You're not going to need it, Kuro. My family isn't against you drinking. You can just use their glasses when you get there."

"But that's my favorite flask!"

"That's because it's your only flask!"

Kuro and Elsa were scrambling to make sure they had everything they needed, while Chris and Silva were standing by the entrance and waiting. Silva had chosen to wear a simple white sundress that day. It went down to her knees, was held up by a simple pair of straps, and revealed a small hint of her cleavage. Of course, Silva was a petite catgirl, so she had small breasts, but this just made her look cute instead of sexy.

"I wish these two were more prepared," Silva muttered with a sigh.

"Expecting them to be prepared is like expecting the sun to rise in the west and set in the east," Chris said.

"I know. I just wish it were otherwise."

Despite the panic from Kuro and Elsa, they did eventually get everything they needed. Their suitcases were packed with clothes, toiletries, and some personal items like laptops, PSPs, reading content, and so on.

Because she was the strongest among them, Kuro carried the suitcases while Chris only carried the smaller bags. He locked the door behind them before they made their way out of the complex and to the bus stop, where they climbed onto a bus that took them to the San Diego Bus Station on Imperial Avenue. Once there, they got onto a megabus on the UC San Diego Blue Line at exactly 8:15 am.

While Silva had ridden on plenty of buses before, she'd never ridden a megabus, which was a massive vehicle with two levels. She marveled at how much bigger the double-decker bus was over the regular buses. She also made a surprised exclamation when she realized there were places to plug in their laptops and other mobile devices. Since she seemed so enamored with everything, Chris let her sit near the window so she could take in the view outside. Kuro sat beside her while Elsa claimed the spot next to him.

Since they were near the front on the upper deck, Silva had a panoramic view of the road as they began traveling. Chris and Elsa pulled out their PSP and began a game of *Monster Hunter*. Meanwhile, Kuro smiled and spoke to Silva as the excited silver-haired catgirl talked about all the things she could see. The smile the wild Amazonian-esque woman gave was amused. It was clear to Chris she was humoring Silva, who had never experienced a long-distance trip like this before.

The trip from San Diego to San Jose was over 11 hours long. The excitement of being on a double-decker bus eventually wore off, and Silva soon laid her head on Kuro's lap, curled up like a cat, and fell asleep. Elsa had also fallen asleep. She rested her head on Chris's shoulder as she lightly dozed off. While Kuro stroked Silva's hair with almost motherly affection (almost because there was no way her feelings for Silva could ever be considered motherly considering the things she'd done to the other catgirl in bed), Chris held one of Elsa's hands and rubbed the back of her hand with his thumb.

"Kids these days, huh?" Kuro said, chuckling at her own joke. Silva was twenty years old, which made her the second oldest person among them. Only Kuro was older at twenty-eight.

"You can't blame Silva for getting so excited she wore herself out," Chris said, also smiling.

"I guess not." Kuro looked out the window for a moment, her cheeks growing a shade darker. "To be honest, I'm a little excited myself. I don't know. Maybe the idea of meeting my mate's family is getting to me too."

Kuro, despite being the most experienced among his catgirls, had never been a catpanion before him. Until her capture at the hands of Markus Flint, she had used Breeders when she needed someone to scratch an itch.

"Just be careful when you meet my family," Chris said.

"Why? Do your parents not like muscular women?" asked Kuro.

"That's not it." Chris shook his head. "My parents might be shocked, but they'll adore you. The problem is my brother." When Kuro just stared at him, he sighed. "He has a thing for women with muscles. I'm worried he might try something."

"Ah." Kuro grinned, showing off her sharp canines. "Don't worry about that. Now that I've chosen to be your catpanion, I won't let anyone else touch me. If he tries anything, I'll put him in his place."

"That's what I'm worried about," Chris muttered, but Kuro just laughed his words off.

They didn't arrive in San Jose until late in the evening, when the sun was setting, casting the sky in a reddish-orange glow. Silva and Elsa had woken up a few hours before then. After the bus stopped at the San Jose bus station on Stover Street between South Montgomery Street and Cahil Street, they called for an Uber to take them to Chris's home, which was another half-hour drive.

"So this is your house?" Silva asked as she, Chris, Elsa, and Kuro stood in front of a simple two-story house in the middle of a residential district. It had a gabled roof, several windows, and a three-car garage. "I don't know why, but I think I was expecting something bigger."

Chris chuckled. "Are all your hopes dashed?"

"Not at all." Silva smiled. "This place looks cozy."

"It's bigger than our apartment," Kuro said as she hefted all three of their suitcases over her shoulders.

"Nya ha ha! Our home is a lot bigger on the inside than it appears on the outside," Elsa boasted.

"Come on," Chris said as he walked up to the front door.

The catgirls followed behind him. He pressed the doorbell and heard a soft chime come from inside. No one seemed to say anything as they waited. Elsa bounced on the balls of her feet, Silva shifted close to Chris and grabbed his sleeve, while Kuro became stone-faced as a cold sweat broke out on her skin.

"Oh, come on. Don't be so nervous," he said to them.

"I'm not nervous," Silva said. "I'm just anxious."

"That's the same thing." Chris rolled his eyes.

"I don't get nervous," Kuro added.

"Say that when you aren't sweating from nerves."

As the playful banter continued, soft thumps echoed from the other side before the sound of a lock being undone reached them. The door opened, and a middle-aged woman with crow's feet, a few wrinkles from smiling, and brown hair greeted them. She bore a slight resemblance to Chris, though most of his features came from his dad.

"I'm home, Mom," Chris said.

"Welcome home." His mom smiled, though there was a gleam in her eyes as she looked at the people with him. "Now, hurry up and come inside so you can introduce me to your catgirls."

Chris almost sighed. Yeah, that was about what he had expected from his mother. A smile came unbidden to his face as he walked inside with the others and began introducing the two nervous catgirls—Kuro and Silva—to his mother.

It was good to be home.

Fin

Afterword

Don't you love a happy ending?

We have now reached the end of Catgirl Doctor 3, and with it, the series is finished. I know your time is precious, but I'd like to take a quick moment to ask everyone who enjoyed this series to please leave a review. Reviews are the life blood of a book and are necessary for an author's continued survival.

With that out of the way, I hope you'll let me talk about Catgirl Doctor for a bit.

My original intention for this series had been to write something cute and erotic. Using Nekopara as my inspiration, I was gonna write a story about one man, several catgirls, and a lot of cute and sexy moments. That idea somehow spiraled into this mixture of dark themes with light-hearted moments, but I think I accomplished my overall goal.

Looking back at my writing, I feel like the protagonist for this story wasn't Chris Redford at all but Silva. She's the character who grew the most throughout this series. She went from a victim of sexual abuse with survivor's guilt and an intense fear of men, to a confident young woman who awakened to her own sexuality and was capable of mastering her fears.

I think the point where I realized Silva was the character who had grown the most was near the end. Mr. Valentine had been clearly hitting on her and making her uncomfortable, but she still managed to confront him about it and express her honest feelings. And her efforts were rewarded since Mr. Valentine was an understanding individual.

Mr. Valentine is actually a counterbalance to Markus Flint. Markus was an abusive asshole, so I wanted to show that Chris wasn't the only good guy in the world. There are more people than the MC who can be good people. Call me naïve, but I like to think most people are inherently good.

With this, the series has come to an official end. Before I go, I would like to give some thank yous to the people who helped make this series possible.

First, I would like to thank Abby for helping me edit and proofread this series. I think she did a pretty good job.

I also want to thank Liremi for doing the artwork. Her art is stellar, truly some of my favorite art of all time. Her style is sexiness wrapped with an extra layer of kawaii, and I love it.

Lastly, I would like to thank all of you. Yes, you. The people who read this series from start to finish. You're all awesome beans. I mean that. None of this would have been possible without your support. I am only here because you are here. Thank you so much for buying, reading, and reviewing this story. It means the world to me.

While Catgirl Doctor is done, that doesn't mean my days of Slice-of-Life fiction are over. If enough people enjoyed this, I was thinking I can write small SoL trilogies. Since these stories don't have much in the way of plot, they would never go beyond a trilogy, but let me with a review that you want more series like this, and I'll do my best to deliver. I was thinking my next SoL series can be about dragon girls.

~Brandon Varnell

Like manga? Brandon is adapting his American Kitsune light novel series into a manga on Patreon!

American Kitsune

I LOVE YOU
I LOVE YOU, TOO.

Haa~
I WISH THAT STUPID ALARM CLOCK COULD HAVE BEEN SILENT FOR JUST FIVE MORE MINUTES. MAYBE THEN I COULD HAVE GOTTEN THAT KISS ...

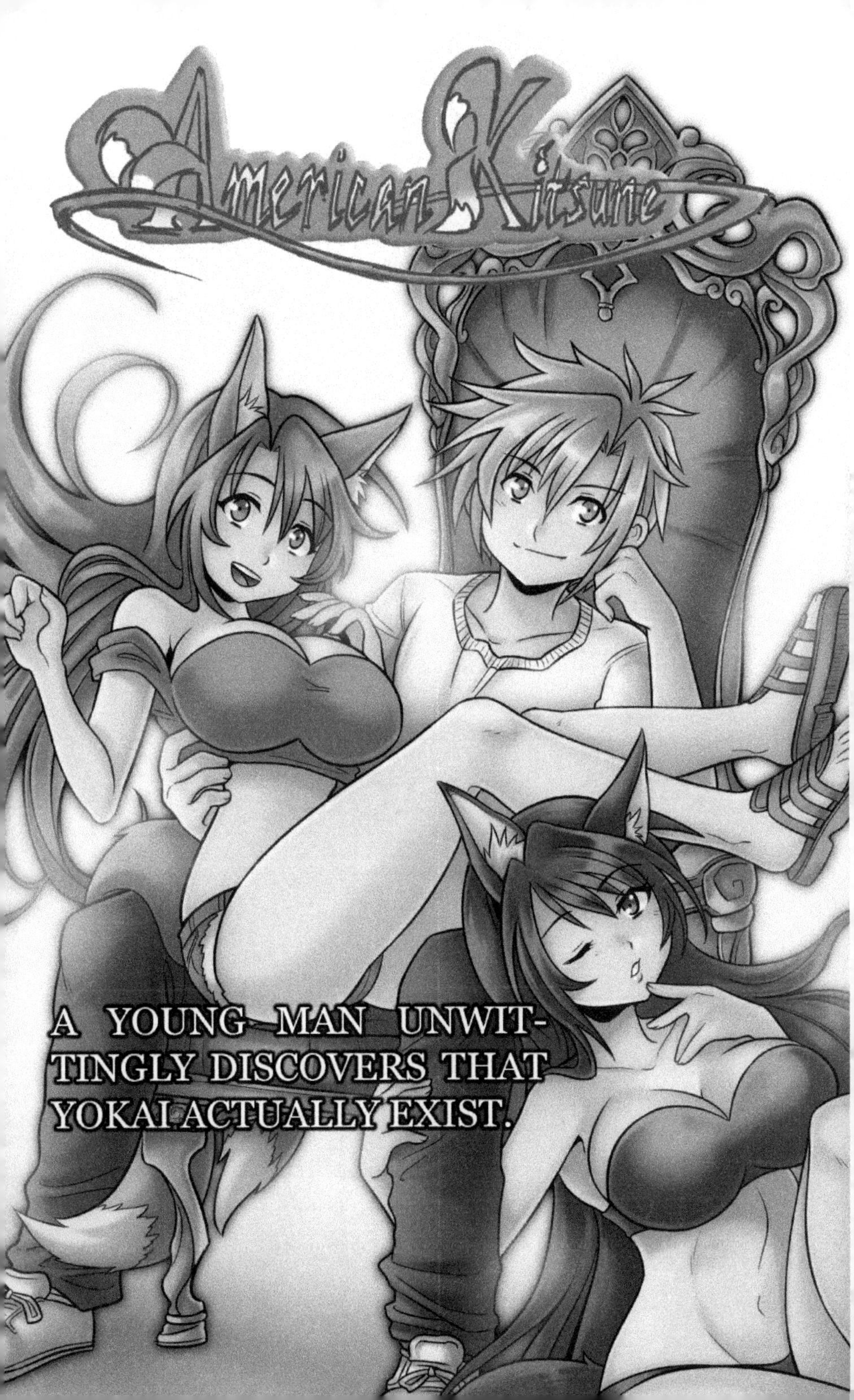
American Kitsune
A YOUNG MAN UNWIT-
TINGLY DISCOVERS THAT
YOKAI ACTUALLY EXIST.

WIEDERGEBURT
LEGEND OF THE REINCARNATED WARRIOR
HE RETURNED TO THE PAST IN ORDER TO CHANGE THE FUTURE.

A MAN DESPERATE TO SAVE HIS LOVER JOINS FORCES WITH A WOMAN LOOKING FOR A WAY OUT OF AN UNWANTED MARRIAGE.
MAN MADE GOD

catgirl doctor
THE STORY OF A YOUNG DOCTOR-IN-TRAINING AND CATGIRLS.

INCUBUS
VERTICAL
THE WORLD'S ONLY INCUBUS
MUST BOND WITH SEVEN
WOMEN!

He just wanted to be a hero.
She didn't want to be stuck in a loveless marriage.
A Most Unlikely Hero

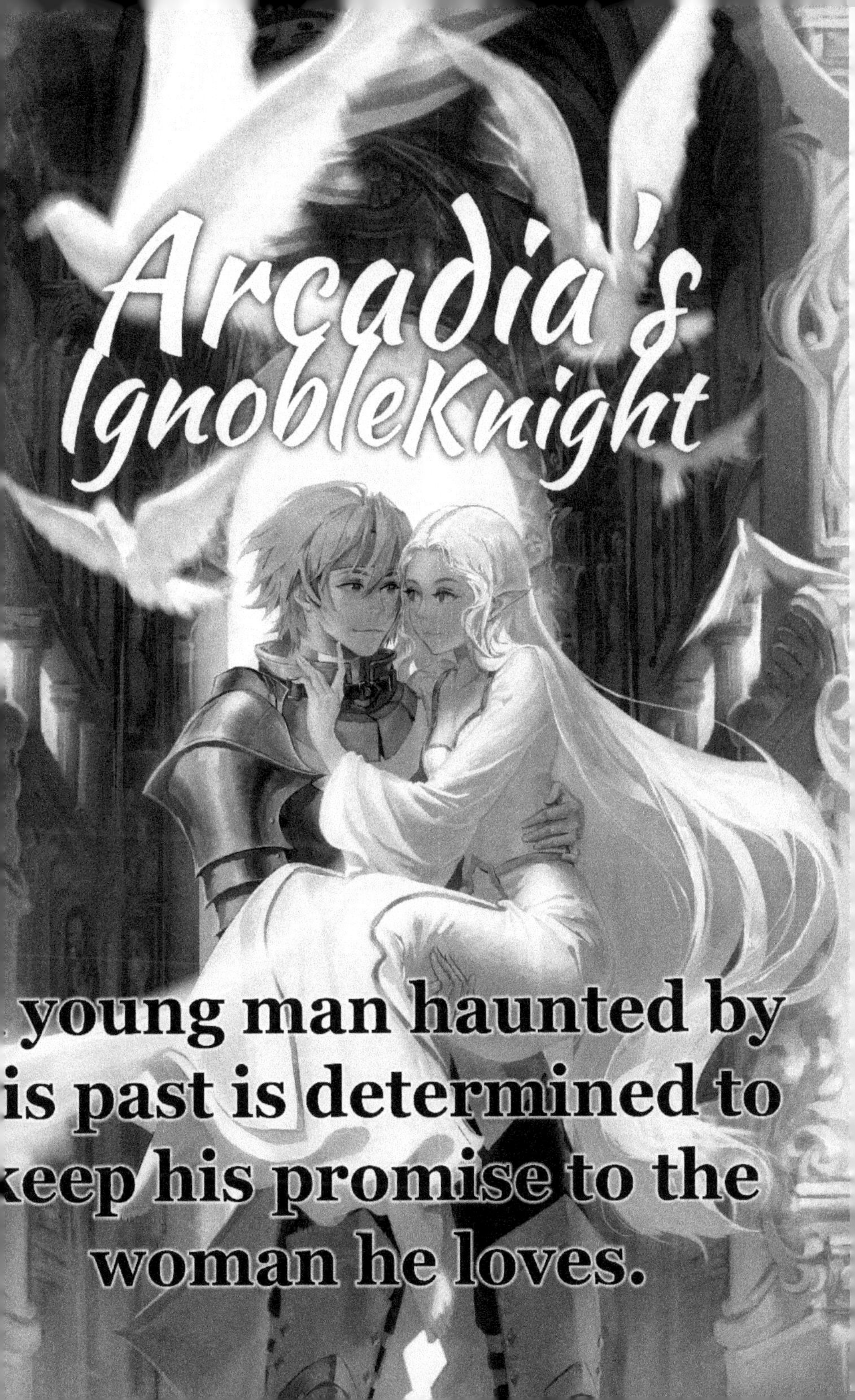

Arcadia's IgnobleKnight
young man haunted by
is past is determined to
keep his promise to the
woman he loves.

A hero betrayed...
A princess dethroned...
These two will join forces....
All for the sake of finding
a place to call home
JOURNEY of a BETRAYED HERO

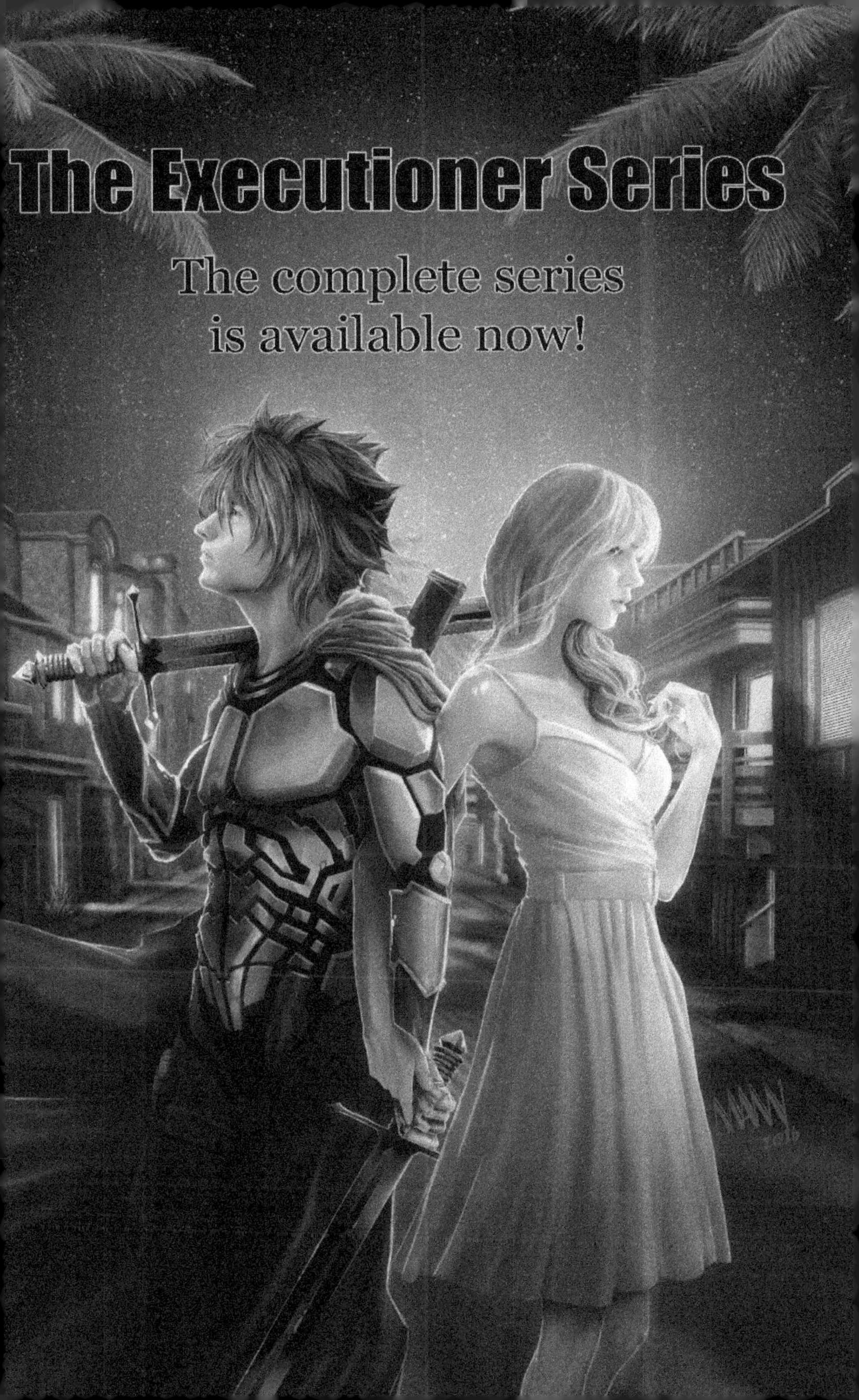
The Executioner Series
The complete series
is available now!

Want to learn when a new book comes out?
Follow me on Social Media!

 @AmericanKitsune

 +BrandonVarnell

 @BrandonBVarnell

 http://bvarnell1101.tumblr.com/

 Brandon Varnell

 BrandonbVarnell

 https://www.patreon.com/
BrandonVarnell